I0678707

Introduction

Children are growing up in a dangerous place. War is taking place outside our windows right in our face. Humans are living in inner cities and ghetto slums, killing each other over crumbs. A small kid asked, "Why is this experiment taking place in my backyard?"

A young kid hides beneath his bottom bunk bed. Wild thoughts going through his head. The child creeps below the window to escape the sound of gunshots, heavy traffic and intense conversation and what not. Voices scattered randomly throughout the night. He slept on the edge of the bed by the door in fright. Cold and afraid. Home alone holding his scroll. Waiting for his mother to come home.

Out of nowhere, an interstellar scientist punched a code into an interface touch screen that powered a weird looking fish bowl. Da Kozmoz had to restart. A new journey to save Invisible Energy's heart. A very special journey to save his future Y chromosome from the dark. Future generations were waiting for a Sol on Marz! Drowning beyond the stars. The next poetic movement demonstration began with no hesitation. Minds opened up beyond education expectations to the poetry in motion invasion.

Gravity had a mission to complete on Mother Earth. Raise five chosen souls from birth, Invisible Energy first. From Marz to Mother Earth. Friendly dark energy connecting all chemistry. The son of Gravity magically gets saved from a tragedy & life in all worlds goes on casually. After ever happily...

Once upon a rhyme, the pen had a best friend. They made line for line again and again. A spiritual design. It was a miracle, a blessing from the skies. The Gods have aligned new information in disguise. The Great Awakening all the planets formed a perfect line......

Da Kozmoz said, "Look, Gravity you're not done writing rhymes till you write a book, your majesty. Stir fry ya mind. Let your thoughts simmer, then serve ya thoughts for dinner. Keep cruising through space on this blue ship like a Buick or a cruise ship. Just have prudence and keep improving. You are so enthusiastic, spoken word music is magic. Keep preaching your own teachings, no need to keep it top secret. Is it under your own pretense? Or a space alien conspiracy theory, reaching frequent angels and demons?"

Gravity replied, "It just happens! This is written in the same fashion, a space mashup. I'm the Gravitational Pull master!"

"We found the perfect position in the sky that gave the planet cosmic waves in 1985. Each child in the womb was given the secrets to the alien tomb, on the darkside of the moon. This energetic collision changed the cosmic positions, upsetting the cosmic musician, compromising the universal orchestra in the fourth dimension. Time is the distance traveled to a place in space. Most people can't remember how they became a member of something so great.

To live is to exist within the galactic orbit. The universe is one galaxy marble clashing against another fantastic forfeit. Cosmic stardust flows within we. The Parallel Universe hides in poetry," Da Kozmoz said.

"With Invisible Energy & Gravity as the Soul specimens of my new science project. It is time to connect the Parallel Universe to Da Kozmoz's fishbowl. A pure entanglement between the two can't be denied. It's the Gravitational bloodline!" Great Grandmother Universe replied.

Cosmic mathematicians travel slow. Ahead of the task of calculating a hidden signal in a new law of physics. Brainwaves are built from the position of Mother Earth during an interstellar light transmission. Many childbirths received the galaxy's frequencies from the Alien Indigo seed. A new species that leads to connecting and respecting the solar breeze. The Parallel Universe speaks, spins, breathes, it's you, it's me!

"Eyes are windows to the soul. Melanin is gold. This is getting old," Da astrophysicist whispers as *he types in a code. [dakozmoz.com] were the keys he typed in. Life as we know it began. A restart on the same simulation. Just for the sake of research on wave equations & different behaviors! A small task in Da Lab of cosmic creators!*

Da Kozmoz Publishing Presents

"Da Kozmoz"

Poetic Motion from the Stars

(The End is The Beginning)

Written by

Gravity Gravitational Pull

Copyright 2-22-2022
Text Copyright © 2022 by MT
GravityMarketPlace LLC / Da Kozmoz Publishing
All rights reserved solely by the author. The author
guarantees all content is original and does not infringe
upon any other person or work. The views expressed in
this book are not necessarily those of the publisher. No
part of this publication may be reproduced, stored in a
retrieval system, or transmitted in any form by any
means, electronical, mechanical, photocopying,
recording, or otherwise, without written permission of the
publisher.

For information regarding permission please contact
Da Kozmoz Publishing online @
dakozmoz.com
dakozmoz@gmail.com

Library of Congress Cataloging-in-Publication Data

LCCN: 2022930506 (print)

ISBN: 979-8-9854408-9-8   (paperback)
Edition Number 222

First edition, February 22, 2022

Dedications

I would like to thank my Aunt Brenda Rogers a.k.a The Poetic Messenger. May she rest in peace. She helped make my dream become a reality. She inspired me and gave me the courage to continue chasing my goals. Without me hearing her strong voice on that last phone call we had, none of this would be possible. Thank You for believing in me more than I believed in myself. I did it Aunty, I wish you were here to witness my success. I know you're watching from up above, sleep in peace. Thanks for the love my heavenly angel.

Dedicated to the future of Poetry

I dedicate this book to my; beloved children Izrael, Nah'mer, Mar'heem, Kwaliyah and Emeri.
Special shout out to my sister Mia, my parents Trudy & Kool Cuzz. To all my family & friends, my loving Godmother Ms.Gwenn. Last but not least, my best friends till the end, Top Knotch / Big Proph /

Judeau Da Planet / Da Kosmic Shooter & Jade Da Goddess.

Table of Contents

"Gravitational Pull!"

The Poetic Movement!

Introduction

Children are growing up in a dangerous place. War is taking place outside our windows right in our face. Humans are living in inner cities and ghetto slums, killing each other over crumbs. A small kid asked, "Why is this experiment taking place in my backyard?"

THE POETIC MOVEMENT!

A young kid hides beneath his bottom bunk bed. Wild thoughts going through his head. The child creeps below the window to escape the sound of gunshots, heavy traffic and intense conversation and what not. Voices scattered randomly throughout the night. He slept on the edge of the bed by the door in fright. Cold and afraid. Home alone holding his scroll. Waiting for his momma to come home.
Traffic whizzed by it was time. The doorknob finally turned as keys jiggled. He ran out of the room and giggled.

Momma said, "Why aren't you in bed?"
"I. I. I was waiting for you Momma," He stammered as he answered.

It was early in the morning. The birds sang as the dawn came in. A cool breeze blew in the door. He wrote a little more. [Noises in the dark, screams from the park.] An audience of sunrays on the windowpane spelled out his name. A sparkling flame of sunlight gave him relief from the night.

Momma yelled, "Here is the broom, get some rest. Later on, clean your room and do your best! I gotta work another double! Dinner is in the oven. Stay out of trouble! Now give me some lovin."

He ran to his bed and jumped in. She kissed him on his forehead again. He got under his sheets.

She hugged him and said, "Don't speak."

She pulled him out of the covers. Looked him up, down and all around. As soon as she was about to speak, she frowned.

He screamed, "Momma, I Know!"

The title was born. He knew what Momma thought. It was on Momma headed off to work. It was time to claim his turf, get into the zone. He knew what to do at home alone.

He shouted, "If the devil ever knocked I never let him in the door! Yeah Momma, I Know!"

A radiant glow formed around his scroll. His eyes glowed. He witnessed the future through his eyes inside his future mind. He started a galaxy within himself. Hope, dreams, truth, honor, bravery, struggle, love, life, death, past, present, future and birth. He was ready for what was offered by Mother Earth.

Momma knew that he had a plan of learning in his own way and keeping himself safe. Another sunrise rotational shift of night turning into day was clearly on its way. Lost in a limbo, he witnessed the sunrays arrive over his window. Approximately eight minutes after they escaped the nuclear fusion of the Sun's surface. A new rotation came as he wrote with a purpose.

"I Know"

Back at it from the top attic, living above jam streets was like a bad habit. I Can't breathe, I'm asthmatic. Too much polluted traffic. Momma said I Can't leave. No return, no keys. This is my therapeutic music exclusively executed better than Newton. In Da Lab, I bake the next movement. Practice my acoustics with human barracudas grooving. You stupid using same old hits as new music. You losing, Gravity is secluded from your view kid! Pure invisible fluids, no pollutants evolve mutants. Problem solved. Rubik's. The Sun Goddess, one unit exclusive to humans. Sunrays distributed like fuel in a Buick. Tell me, why are you waiting? There are no excuses, just do it! Careful how you use it. Da Kozmoz without Gravity is undisputed! What are you doing? Space station cruising? They hating but they are rooting. This is really true, isn't it? New music always needs real improvement. The beginning is the conclusion. Gravity born attuned with solar fusion and you have been confused since the delusion. You have been confused since the delusion! The Universe will always even the score! If the devil ever knocks, I never let him in the door! Poem 1.

One glimpse of himself in the mirror, he was alive. The energy could take him everywhere but there. He could do anything he dared. His Imagination broke barriers. Without ever leaving his room, he roamed new areas. Momma didn't have to worry. He knew how to create his own reality if things got scarier.

A voice in his head whispered, "Gravity Gravitational Pull is your soul carrier."

Existence of the Parallel World has shown itself inside his dome. Gravity left Mothership once again and finally made it home. Gravity has awakened in a six-year-old human wardrobe.

Sirens blared past the window, so he closed it and turned the TV on, looking for a good show. Flicking through the few channels he had, he found nothing to make him laugh. Nothing but pointless shows of phony messages and lies. He couldn't find anything entertaining. The news showed all the homicides. Finally, on the Diablo network there was a hidden lesson. The history of enslaved African Americans caught his attention. It was the opening of a new dimension.

He thought out loud, "Who's fault is it Momma has to work all day and hustle? Who am I to blame for our misfortunate life struggles? This isn't a game!"

At the age of six, the struggle of the everyday hustle wasn't his fault. Right outside the window, on the sidewalk, two guys fought. The sirens came back louder and louder. The guys ran off like cowards. He texted Momma from behind the couch, hiding for hours. He wrote a poem.

"Who's 2 Blame?"

European ways colonized our bodies, souls & brains. First whips and chains, now it's cheap thrills, gold and fame. Who's 2 blame? Your self consciousness that allowed you to do the nonsense. Who's 2 blame? You been dumb down ever since you believed you only used ten percent of ya brain. Who's 2 blame? Religious beliefs or violent streets. B-L-A-M-E the hate, blame the heat, blame the fake, blame the blame, cause without the who is you. It's all the same. Who's 2 blame? Poem 2.

Momma replied, "I will be home soon, hopefully. Go to your room and write more poetry. I'm off tomorrow night supposedly."

When Momma had the night off, the back door stayed open. She spent her time in the kitchen talking on the phone joking. She prepared a delicious dinner meal. She knew how to cheat in her weekly card game and win with wheels. All her friends started coming over.

She said, "Come on in tonight, I'm luckier than a four leaf clover."

After we ate, Momma and her company played cards for hours. She and her partner Mr.White, the neighborhood mechanic, had all the power.

She said, "It's cutthroat time!"

Cutthroat was the same game, but more treacherous. No partners, every man for themselves. Sounds kind of selfish.

She said, "Put up or shut up!"

Mr. White put his share up. Miss Sandy from next door rolled her eyes and watched Momma win. She had a good night again.

Pop-Pop was on his way. He always came on card day. He played pinochle every week with his cousin Preston. Spades were like Go fish to them. Momma and Mr. White partnered up against Pop-Pop and Miss Sandy from next door. Pop-Pop gave him a wink and a grin as he held his cards in his hand. Momma let him keep score. He sat next to Momma, and wrote a little more notes.

"Spades"

Ace of hearts, Momma, play your part. Let's look for the next book to get dark. Straight from the door cutting gets Pop-Pop shook. He wishes he went board. Deuce a diamond deuce spade. Now I'm counting cards. Chop city. I'm like not really. Pop-Pop went for wheels. That sounds silly. Momma holds it down South Jersey and out Philly. Clubs get no love, diamonds chilly. Frogs hop on lily! It's not what you thought, really! Momma, your team is shot! Can you hear me? I tried to warn you, don't come around my corner. Your lead is the best lead, scary horror. Pop-pop, rather renege on his own daughter than admit this was a slaughter.

Miss Sandy said, "Us on fire, Them need water!"

Momma said, "What?"

Pop-Pop shouted, "That's a head rub caught you!"
Poem 3.

Pop-Pop gave him a handshake full of winnings. He lived everyday like it was the bottom of the ninth inning.

He said, "This isn't living, it's just the beginning."

Underneath his covers with a flashlight, he counted some ones, and he wrote for fun.

"From Da Door"

Toxic disease blowing in the breeze. I truly believe they are feeding us poisonous seeds. As cannons release in the cold streets, I drop on one knee, accept no apologies' cause my flow is seven seas. May you rest in peace. On these streets, ain't nothing guaranteed. They are onto me. So I creep while they sleep. Pure alien breeds don't breathe. We lead the sheep to peace. Between the lines I read, no need to climb because I peak to the extreme. Higher than alien indigo dreams. Gravity happens naturally. Man, please let it go go go!!! Too late, too slow, slow, slow!!! **Poem 4.**

He had a crush on the mail lady. She came every day like clockwork. She was caring like a hot nurse. He would play his Nintendo and wait in the window with smiles. She was the only person Momma allowed in the house when she was out. He loved that she stopped by all the time. He was home with his scroll & writing lines next to a full figured voluptuous queen of all time. The queen of his heart sat next to him on the throne. Momma's best friend sat in her chair when she wasn't home. She had him in the zone. Mrs. Wise was always around. She always had a letter for whoever crossed her path in town. She was a three moon goddess. She knew her astrologic math. Soon to be the hottest on the map in fact.

Soon after, she finished her break. She backed the mail truck out of Momma's parking spot and told him, "Move to a new chapter. Immerse in the moonlight. It's going to be a full moon tonight and tell Momma I'll see her later. Alright?."

Drowning in her intoxicating scent, he closed his eyes and imagined her still sitting with him. He wished it was real, and she held him close. He howled at the moonlight, opened his eyes, and scribbled as his drool dribbled.

"Full Moon"

Evolve floating to resolve all our commotions in motion half, full or new, I am with you. By your side until doom doom doom or we collide boom boom boom to make room room room for a futuristic me and you. Who considered you seeing it through? When you move, you create wind & high tides. Swirl my world like a spoon. July to June side-by-side til we die you are my moon. My other half in the sky, till I die! **Poem 5.**

He was so in love, so he kept writing.

"Lazer Love"

No worries when a god meets his goddess, all options become
blurry. So rain down your exotic astrologic flurries. Camera lens
focusing fantasy of dreams soaking in. Now we are closer than
friends. By any means, Can I be your new man? Imagine
Holding hands in the sand on jet skis, no pet peeves. I didn't
understand the tricks up your sleeve. You got a man, but I'm
going to keep making plans. Don't think I forgot your jet stream.
Mrs.Wise, you're so hot I would never leave. You're H-O-T
hotter than a block full of cops. I had to stop and watch you
walk out of my life. A shining star so bright concealed out of my
sight. That's not right. Who knows, one day you could be my
wife? I feel like spam trapped in a can because she's a goddess
out of my league. Now I'm on bending knee L-O-V-E at first
sight. Born ready to please your every need. Guaranteed any
night grand slam out the ballpark, bottom of the ninth. This is
what I call art. You could be my second in command, like Jean-
Claude Van Damme. It's never too late for a late start, so slide
your family into home plate. Now you're safe. The penalty is
only five yards. It's getting dark. More scars form across my
heart. I will survive it all with you as my fate that creates love,
not hate. I Write this remedy better than great. For heaven's sake
Time on the outside for you and me. A goddess queen of unity.
We are never enemies. We had a couple of soft drinks. Never
had to tell you how I think. Ever since I imagined our first kiss, I
felt the Earth spin under my feet. All the pain in my past was
well worth it. Living in these crumbling streets under the
surface, with serpents lurking in heat. So I ask you this, will you

be my Mrs.Gravity and live happily? With me? As time drifts, rhyme hits only to wish this is it! Universal bliss on the mothership Brady Bunch a dozen kids. Philly jawn took me to places I had never been gone. Out-of-body experience out of my skin, I'm serious! Amazing goddess creation, I finally win. Body shaking, your love is amazing. Can I harness your energy chemistry? Freedom growth awakens your unique love heals touch builds addictive inspirations. Copper skin, copper eyes, mind hypnotize thighs. We are deeply connected, like overlapping intersections and shared connections. Heavenly blessings! Spell-casting, love notes, love jones and love poems. Love come back home when everything is just right for life in the Goldilocks' Zone. **Poem 6.**

Momma had nothing. She made it through life, bluffing. A crummy one bedroom apartment, a bus pass and the clothes on her back was all she had. She learned the truth at an early age. She read several books every single page. Taking a different look from inside the cage. Encyclopedias to social media from calm to full rage. Momma was just trying to get paid.

Watching television, the little boy was bombarded with a flood riddles. This insane amount of information had him trapped in the middle. Torn between two worlds this and the Parallel. He got played like a fiddle until he chose to compose his own show of wisdom. From years of research, he made things work. He developed a gravitational pull like no other on Mother Earth. Knowledge of self is true belief. Not dollars or wealth on the street. He wrote another note.

"Hidden Wisdom"

The hidden wisdom dwelled within a frequency rhythm. Crawling is living, walking dead isn't. The soul is forgiving. The witness shouldn't be in prison. He could've talked instead. Now the body chalked in from head to toe. The truth has never been said before. Five O' at the door kicking. Now you're missing. The hole you keep digging & digging. With toxins in your liver mixing. Take control of your soul. You must stop it and start living. Remember, your presence is vicious better than Christmas! Gone is still moving on. That's the start of an old ending or end of a new beginning. **Poem 7.**

His hidden wisdom became his religion. When things got rough and the devil started twitching. Banging, knocking and kicking his bowels stayed put as he used invisible forces in full force. To remove any obstacle that obstructed his path. He had always wondered how far he could grasp. With his imagination, the knowledge he was born with took him even farther. Waiting for Momma to come home, he decided to call her. Busy working, she never replied, so he became an author. He started writing from an imaginary location. A rotating space station with universal ancestral neighbors.

He dreamt of a poetic story about the history of our ancestors. It came to him through an ancient DNA code and letters. A connection from the Parallel Universe itself is a grand treasure. His scroll began to glow and his eyes shut. He went aboard a time-traveling train back into time. Ancient times a space where two universes bounced off each other, moving invisible lines. The Interstellar Dimensional RailRoad finally dropped him off at the end. Which was naturally the beginning. As he stood at the end of the railroad. In the center of a black hole, he was told secrets of [Da Kozmoz.] One of Great Grandmother's ancient codes.

"Ancient light years"

These light years goes not quite as it supposed but through it all the seed of the copper skin Martians, has grown full blown. The Sun rose above the horizon. Five minutes to ten. The day was finished. It was the end. Around 1865'ish all the surviving gods & goddesses kept their promise. The DNA is alive & thriving! I repeat, the DNA is alive & thriving! Again, the DNA is alive & thriving! They hid this incident in between hours. A significant dream power. Innocent Indigenous Copper Skin Indians were treated like immigrants. Same dude brain food, it's him again with relish. Developed capabilities to embellish the difference. Are you lost with Gilligan? It's all written, I'm not giving lessons, jest visiting with peasants. Delivering messages with pigeons and pheasants. Sitting on fences till the end of present. It rains pain forever and ever. Gravity will never stop pulling your chain yanking your lever. I left my Sol on Marz. No time to explain. My illuminating lectures glow with the stars. My Left brain contains excruciating weather patterns. Scattered hallucinations share demonstrations. Cloud hopping over waves, closes doors and open gates. We came a long way from older days. If that sounds common, this is no mistake. UFO flying saucer or dinner plate. An ancient flying fire comet will cast over. Enslavement is power, power is control, control is enslavement. At last it's over. At last it's over! Can you hear me now? I'm a sightseer in the ear canal of your right ear. Spirit of life traveling light years to plant a seed right here. Four scores & a quintillion years, I've been chilling here spilling tears. The atmosphere started acting weird. Flashbacks of your past will flash in the mirror. So why are we standing here? Let's put the craft in gear. Why search for outer-space out there? When Mother Earth is outer space right here. Crash landed out of date. Let's take your mind through space time, interstellar fly-by and no painted lines. Attacked with meteorites & asteroids at the same time. Backwards sunrise, upside down thundering skies. Thoughts will be inside out wandering off. Trying to tell you, you are a god? You will witness the purple moonlight. The climate will start rising through the night. The orbit will change rotation, day will flip to night. Mother Earth will start frying like old bacon, the hell planet of satin waiting in the making. At first thought backwards looks pleasant, but instead it's a curse from the heavens. Beyond the limits of physics, your consciousness is living in a solar system made in god's image. The DNA religion generations of bloodline traits, characteristics, faith, tradition, race, ancestral culture, mitochondrial DNA vulture, passed down vulgar. All mothers & daughters must offer the culture and spawn of us no mutation. Moving forward with a thrust towards the doors above a higher dimension. Hopscotch back to planet Rock, Mercury is the Sun's moon exploding soon. Dust will release atmospheric gasses. Mother Earth goes doom on Father Marz life will resume. Hybrid artificial intellectual trans-human, no perfume man, non-gender. When robotic cows are jumping over the moon. Surrender to a universe in a dark room full of colossal crash fumes. Fly away or become consumed into universal black hole tombs. Fly away or become consumed into universal black hole tombs! **Poem 8.**

To be different is to walk alone. Stand out in the crowd. A King on his throne. The needle in the haystack, the diamond in the rough. Flesh and bone. Mentally tough, physically buff, spiritually up, emotionally loved & gravitationally home. A notch above the rest. Enter a new zone, a new quest. Fall back to get ahead. keep pushing forward from the legs.

"I Walk Alone"

Dark forces stay in orbit, invisibility is of great importance. As Gravity, I distort this. Unknown digital recording, unknown location, unknown coordinates. I walk alone in the forest, sitting on my throne dormant. I rise high above the sky, an enormous skyscraper, Air Jordan. No talk on the phone. I'm focused on this poem, this performance. I walk alone forever with pure endurance. Born awoke, never snoring. Pureness with more sense than quarters we spent on corner store water. **Poem 9.**

"On my Job"

I had to turn the page to learn my age. Burn old flames and contain the change. Gravity is the name Da Kozmoz is the claim. I rock shows without a stage. Far from crazy and deranged. They say I'm insane and it delays my skills. They are out of my range! They can't understand that uniqueness is kinda strange. Life is a movie lined up in the frame. I love when night rain floods the streets like my pain floods my cheeks. I keep saying I'm a God again & again ancient bacteria surviving on mud stain globs. Seed planted by my Great Grandmother's job. From the beginning to the end rich in a galactic haze in many fantastic ways. **Poem 10.**

"Ghetto Gotham"

This system design is 3D poverty. You must fall victim to one balance of the galaxy. Location isn't real until a black hole can swallow me. In the Parallel, each universe has a different name because the same place exists on opposite ends. Light took quintillions of years to omit here, check your optical lens. Placed at the bottom of the list like the last sip. Black male, that's it. Don't eat the crab dip. Potions dumb us down. Too many living at a loss can't get jobs, skipping bonds, so it's back to committing frauds, a repeat cycle for cons. There he goes, he just sold his soul in front of a synagogue, anything goes giving the cost. This is not on its off! Raised in a lab like gorilla frogs. Then placed on the pond, we swam, jumped on land, learned to jog with a gun and ran. Isn't this odd? Urban gods are legends embedded in these concrete cages of torture. It's a legend that goes beyond horror, street natural law and order. Unspoken terms never speak too crafty for the cheese recipe. (H double O D) will never be set free, those toys are us Geoffrey. Gladiatorial big warrior abnormal gargoyle brick forester. **Poem 11.**

Pop-Pop was the grim reaper he always spoke of death. All his friends were dying off and fast. There weren't many left, but Pop-Pop wasn't afraid of his future or past.

He said, "Death! Even when you're dead, you're alive in the past!"

The news he carried was sad news. Miss Sandy from next door had passed.

Pop-Pop yelled, "She will live forever through us!"

On that sad day he sat on the bus and wrote; Hey Sandra Wassup?

"Death!"

The body never decays. Grows forever in any stage. After death, it's another step. Process the next quest for the flesh. You may never rest in peace. Bury me in a (H-O-L-E) and let me be. My brain waves will pave ways for a new day in eternal sleep. I learn to be forever accepting no delete. Crows chirping, Grim lurking. Too bad I got a purpose. The game never ends. I transcend through dimensions beyond the grave; I seen it all. Resting in eternity, I dreamed it all. Each life is a free-for-all. A lesson on the streets is what I recall. Let's take a walk outside the chalk, no time to talk, for every slave that didn't behave or shared the master's name, I share this beyond the grave. Thanks for being brave, not dying, not knowing you will be a flying angel with a clean slate crying. Generations free one day, crying tears of freedom. Showing us anything is worth trying for!

Nothing is worth dying for, unless it's for a bigger cost to save our species from extinction like dinosaurs. I have been here before. No lying, it's so surprising my flow is disguised in robotic wiring. The Poetic Movement is serious, like Sirius C Dogon shining. Our life is beyond men; it never ends. Written with no pens. Energy passed down in DNA like blends of chemistry. Remember me so long Miss Sandy. **Poem 12.**

Finally, Momma got a raise, and they moved into a two bedroom across town. Same scenario, different street, same sound. slightly bigger living spaces, same blocks, same faces. Momma still worked six days a week, four doubles and two straight shifts. A few years passed by. He started to notice even more things around him. His poetry seems to help him speak openly. He learned to cope with life's trials and bad dreams & the streets. His gravitational pull helps him more each day. A new imagination was the way. He dreamed of living in his own world. He wanted to be from another planet. Away from the cold nights and hunger pangs. Far away from another universe, somewhere strange. He wished everything would be different. In his new bathroom mirror he entered a different dimension.

"Different topics"

Different topics, all go back to a base derived from the same objects. Surviving outer space in a rocket, I spit hotness. Time isn't logic, when you're beyond clock ticks. Who needs pockets when your brain contains the message from the Sun Goddess. Humans downloaded sunrays on solar panels and created computer animals. Artificial intelligence ricocheted then exploded. Does that sound bogus? I would give it all away if there was no such thing as options. Like living free, not boxed in. Are you feeling me? Forget the nonsense, knowledge only deposits in the most conscious. Too bad most of the populous is toxic, fast asleep, nodding. Suicide, homicide genocide we must never die. We need some different topics to survive the apocalypse. I been alive, plotting on different topics. **Poem 13.**

In the mirror he saw some force rising out of the darkness. A gravitational storm came rolling in like a fire truck parking at a five alarm blaze. Time seemed to stand still yet turn a page. Then acid rain came moving quickly, flashing flames. Thunder and lightning started rumbling. Tomorrow wasn't coming, nor did it exist. He wasn't quite sure what time was. An orbit took time and space to operate. His mind was on a new rotation to cooperate. Each revolution he learned more.
Watching the rain against the windowpane, he wrote some more.

"Tomorrow never dies"

Today is tomorrow. Tomorrow is in the sky. Space traveled between movement is accurate time. Time doesn't live yet never dies, today lives forever in expanding skies. Cosmic clouds of terrible weather move in & move out in all dimensions. Without a sound. In all directions out of bounds. Gravity holds you down unannounced. Gravitational Pull! The Poetic Movement explodes across the globe underground! Who wants it now? Now you wonder how? Dark energy is the universal DNA chemistry and cosmic stardust combust connecting us genetically. **Poem 14.**

Peeking out the window, He saw cameras on the traffic lights. Cameras on the telephone poles connected to the corner store. People walked by with cameras on their phones riding hub boards, taking selfies acting like they were wealthy. He felt he had to get stealthy. In pajamas jamming cameras. They all started moving in his direction, zooming in, zooming out, no detection. The cameras were watching him. A birdseye, above the curbside, couldn't see what's in his third eye. He heard a bang, tire squealed and boom a car crashed. Instantly, everything that just happened so fast. Outside his window was playing live on blast. Online live, cameras had cameras for girls and guys. Streams flooded the scene. His mind drifted somewhere else. He thought the forces were closing in on him. He crawled under the bed.

Whispering to himself he said, "They're Watching!"

"They're Watching!"

Eagle eyes saw my disguise, living hidden inside. I recently realized I'm living a lie. This land disadvantaged the black man. Black targets in a gun range, the Black Man. I'm a dragon spitting fire, running from pain, leaving blood stains. Whips skidding tires. This artificial world is getting critically strange. Invisible chains holding brains, controlling souls & other things. They are coming, man! They saw you coming a mile away. So you better slide away to your honeycomb hide away. Try going off the grid. Don't jump off a bridge or slit your wrist. This is it, the cost to live, welcome to the system, foster kid! You can't get punked and risk it all. Play the game, kick the ball, this is war! Take what's yours. They looked at us under a microscope writing notes. Gravity stays moving in the shadows like light smoke. The slightest hope at the highest dose widens my scopes. Cameras on a light pole high as tight ropes. Gravity is quite dope! **Poem 15.**

He stayed under the bunk bed with his back against the floor and his pencil to paper, his paper against the bed. To the sound of traffic zipping by, laying upside down, he kept on writing. He wrote with hope his notes did the fighting.

"Back against the Parallel World"

Robins and jays flying above a maze while I'm paving my way through traffic. Wish I was at a picnic chasing bread baskets. Transmissions slipping, sticking, not shifting. Now I'm causing accidents. The walking dead driving caskets. Forget this world & all its contents. Continents full of unconscious monsters. Gravity is dominant, so pass the pasta man! Spark that fire in the sand, forget a traffic jam. No drinking and driving, not sure about pulling over. Only drive sober, never ride the shoulder. The time is over fam. You're submissive to the mind controller. They want your soul soldier, your life is over. Life is not what they told us. Fruit can't roll up as such. That's nuts, big as posters. If life is poker, watch out I got the big joker! (PAUSE) Out the window it's a holdup! As soon as the corner store opened up dude double pumped the smoker. Looked at Mrs.Kim and smoked her!

Her Husband dropped to the floor holding her and said, "Take what you want!" trouble jumped on my mind now I'm focused, poem over. Never drink and drive. Never text and drive. Poems are words that never risk our lives. **Poem 16.**

He always dreamed of leaving this planet. He dreamed of leaving the panic. Invading planets, solar systems and galaxies! He loved to escape this madness of a place. Everyday violence screams. The hood shouldn't be so passive. No anti-black violence is active. If it is ain't nothing happening. Cities across the country are death traps for our youth. It's obvious we need a truce. A deal to end street warfare going everywhere. A crime takes place every second in America! When will we clear it up and not tear it up?

A quick drift to another planet he spoke.

"Accidental Invasion"

I accidentally landed on this hell planet frantic. No need to panic, I'm Martian and I understand it. Now back to your daily programming. Holding hands with a philanthropist. The mission is to create division. Holy ghost dancing mix. Unorganized religion is scamming like crooked politicians. Out for the grip. Disguise and hide behind the unruly decision. The Earth is spinning with electromagnetism flips. Bear witness to this Gravitational Pull! No position close your eyes envision a fresh way of living. Open your eyes and take the risk. Get out of this! **Poem. 17**

Momma was home from her shift early one day. She had a surprise! She told her son to get dressed and be ready to love life. She walked him down to the corner and they made a right. Into a brown door. Some man stood tall with a dark shadow on the floor. The man looked at him and cried. He didn't know why this guy had tears in his eyes. A grown man was crying.

Momma was trying to say, "This is your father, I'm not lying."

His life changed forever that day.
His father handed him a note and it read the love life letter.

"Love Life Letter"

You must love life, and life will love you. River streams grow in between dust openings in the land of dreams. I'm not a man, I'm a being, I gleam. I go extreme glow and beam elite supreme complete life schemes on repeat no disease. Just holding golden keys to a second universe beyond overseas. Open your mind. You know what I mean? The second brain envisions a sound wave like hieroglyphics found in a cave. Megahertz trembles the Earth with treble as my words. Bass shot down from space reality you must face. Before it's too late, meditate to elevate your mind state. Just another rose thorn grown in the concrete ground. Born king without a crown on these concrete streets. Sworn in with vowels: die or go to jail or throw in the towel. Don't get shipped to school and never found or be stripped of mental jewels! That's plantation bound. Man, you are facing it now! Different tools, same style old soul capture rituals passed down. Aboriginal indigenous participants left frozen in the cold shivering. Top of the totem pole chopped off by militants. Who also sold their soul for the cost to live. Blinded by the cross eyed demons stripped of all beliefs screaming. They were quick to call me chief Indian not (K-I-N-G). That's sickening to me. They claim they came in peace but they were whispering,

"Idiots savage copper skin beasts are considered hideous. Let's lock them in with corrupt police & get them boxed in with disease begging please on their knees!"

Is it Thanksgiving again? I feel a nose bleed. There was no

feast, just insidious affiliates that raped our innocence. No peace, nothing to eat. Floods of immigrants look like distant cousins came chained on ships. All this oblivious blood covers the streets. Our current living predicaments are not a coincidence. We were drowning then and now it hits again. Drowning with the devil sizzling. Trapped in these ghettos are physical imprisonment. Sixty cent is a decimal with separate equivalence. Who legislates its citizens standing on a pedestal to implement? The rain comes down from the clouds with infinite stimulants. Brain plays instruments. My mind is intricate and adds spice like cinnamon. It gets inclement every increment. If you are not digging this cause, you are not living it. Camping on the side of the road, in a tent, or under a bridge is where our homeless live. A slave to the game called tradition. Stop smoking & drinking. Start hoping and thinking. I eat knowledge when I'm hungry and there's no dinner. True kings do things: no games, no winners. Groundhog predicting winter sounds fraud like Christmas in December. Pretenders give plenty of members live agendas. I live forever, they tell lies forever driving Teslas. I'm happy to be alive after surviving breakfast. Every second they aim weapons after our melanin copper skin element. The truest crown of all developments is the Martian settlement. My universal soul connected like legos to some strange Interdimensional Railroad. This extraterrestrial gave my DNA a head full of scrolls. They came for a feast, so I gave them a festival of gold. **Poem 18.**

Nice to meet you son. Sorry I wasn't around but I got caught with a gun. My skin was black so I had to run. Time served in jail is no fun. Never thought I would live to see you kid. It is what it is. This is it. When my world started turning worse. I realized I didn't want to leave you with a stress burden curse. So your Momma made it work. That may have been the wrong thing but I went away before your birth. Before I left, I gave your Momma all I had. It was enough to get you two a starter pad. You have grown into an incredible force. Keep staying positive and believe, and one day you will succeed. I love you of course. Yours truly, your Dad!

His dad spoke to him about playing catch, getting to know him and things he wanted to show him. The words he spoke showed him he loved him. The "Love Life Letter" revealed some hidden answers above him. He needed these ancient secrets to complete his thesis. His mom never mentioned his dad before this day.

One day which happened to be on Sunday. He knew he would meet him someway someday. He felt inside that he was alive, that's it the rest was a surprise.

He finally had a real audience besides the Sun, Earth & moon. He was no longer standing staring at the walls in his room. His parents knew that inside their son Gravity grew. He performed in laundromats, check cashing places, and bus stops all across town. His voice created soundwaves across any room. No one believed what a boy his age knew. He realized how important frequencies were and used them to his ability. Started building his own reality. With his words he would carry frequencies. Inside his eyes was a glowing soul. On the way back home he wrote in his growing scroll.

"Soundwaves"

Humans weren't first on this Earth or universe. Full of vast energy sources, and we use fossil fuels like fools to make faster Porsches. Went from pigeon mail carrier to video chat cell carrier. What's next? You can teleport your voice to break the sound barrier. With any device of your choice, which sounds scarier? Solar nuclear tsunami wave or radiation radio wave traveling through space? Both could wipe out an entire race. I telecommunicate my transformation is how I transport my information. Abroad in one door and out the next. I found a fresh way to teleport beyond text. Soundwaves originated from pulsar stars eons away. Compressed energy passed invisibly, yet physically, from quest to quest. Gravitational forces, I just teleported from my last death yes yes! Its sound waves you know where to find me nowadays, I must be eternal in this inferno. I never found my grave. **Poem 19.**

Thoughts became the first step toward his goals. So he spoke thoughts out loud.

"Been Here Before You"

Forced in this orbit like a cosmic sponge, I absorb it or plunge. First organism born with wisdom and lungs. In this portal system we crumbs. Sea cell transported to land forest by sea shell. Before slave ships, hurricanes rode different waves. They are still paving a way for pain buried away. See what we are living in today? Is it a result from yesterday? From amphibian to man, birth from sunrays. Ancient sprays from solar gunplay made man. Understand? Gravity displays indigenous ways, written in aboriginal Martian native caves. **Poem 20.**

Momma became head nurse. She deserved it from all her hard work. Things started looking better for Momma. She didn't have to slave as many hours. She made more money. The second she got the promotion, their bags were in motion. No jokes, nothing was funny. She put a down payment on a new house. Finally, our own home in the country, far out. Moving up wasn't our destination, we were moving down but not south, down to Earth not a route.

Meanwhile, Momma baked a fresh apple pie. Her little guy sat in the window seat of the new place and dropped a beat on her suitcase. The acoustics were amazing. The truth is he wasn't famous, but the view tamed his anger. No more arguments and shots of danger. No more bullets, no more strangers. No more crime murder or drugs. No more danger, plenty more love.

"Window Seat"

Fresh out the cage in my mind. We finally escaped the system design. Free to breathe, free to inhale the breeze. Outside the treeline over the sea, we fly. Out of this world over the street wide awoke far from sleep we fly. Over the nonsense from unconscious violent sheep zombies. I'm beyond the horizon shining light years and still rhyming. I know why the caged birds sing, trapped in a maze. My words are my wings. Each phrase is made for kings and queens. We outside your window flying in a limo you ain't seeing things take your head off the pillow. **Poem 21.**

For a second he thought he was going crazy. He didn't realize his true reality was hazy. He spoke of this amazing culture being invaded by an unidentified species of giant alien vultures.

"Krazy"

Escaping to Mother Earth as a space station was my first equation. My unknown alien nation was facing immigration. My family was being separated. I'm a contaminated, contagious atheist born, awakened on a vacation alien location Marz equator. I spot wavelengths and hear vibrations. Just to clear my patients, I get high with vibrations. Never too complacent. I spent a day's length in time. As the stars went by, my heart started racing. Inside the basement, I'm back and forth pacing. Gravitationally waiting, building a foundation. If you think it's crazy. Might just turn out it's amazing. Krazy how the Martians reversed the invasion with an escape to Mother Earth space station equation. **Poem 22.**

In the beginning hip hop was a nonviolent purity of one's consciousness. A view from a caged animal on the curbside before contactless-pickup. The game has changed since Wu-Tang. He wrote that real men never give up.

"The Revolution of Hip Hop"

We evolved hip hop to resolve problems suggesting a solution from gang shootings. A revolt on our own people. We will never be equal! The big bang made the first beat continuously on repeat. Kids hang on the wrong street hip hop since hieroglyphics scripts in tombs like Nefertiti to graffiti on walls of brick. Tv cd dvd to this. Started back on Similac.

The stick up kid said, "Give me that! This is armed robbery!"

Young God bodies on the corner drinking, living in poverty, not thinking. Knowledge in rhymes had me wondering. Hip hop philosophy is our revolution against inequality. The government doesn't love this, they just publishing. Call us a crook, if you booked or wrote a book, either you are struggling or you are in this suffering. The revolution of hip hop made a pit stop on all blocks. Running from the cops never interfered with the music in our ears. Hip started running laps. Hop started running it back. First created stats of something that was never just black. A mixture of all music combined with rhymes. The first of its kind. Brain waves in position to brainstorm a new vision. The great escape. Our way to getaway, before slavery we did it the same way. We used music as a way to rebel against the spell. Separate still till this day, we don't hesitate to use our music to elevate. I'm growing against the fence like a rose in the cement growing bent product of my environment, which you can't make sense of. From spray paint to Gravity the godly saint. The evolution of hip hop, our revolution within a revolution, an escape from execution. Africans brought over on ships and stripped of native origins. Then mixed with copper skin Indians. Religions forced in given nothing but unfair portions. Men hung as the slaves sung hymns during worship. Ever since 110 years after the south was overthrown. We finally had something to call our own. From break dancing, beatbox, DJ's & battle shows into Da lab out came cultural growth! Da Kozmoz **Poem 23.**

He has evolved alongside a humongous force. He grew taller and stronger, of course. Gravity Gravitational Pull couldn't stay hidden any longer. It was time to teleport, the only way to feed his intellectual hunger. Above the clouds on his magic carpet, he became the smartest. No doubt he had the power of hidden wisdom within. His mitochondrial DNA held him down alongside his Y chromosomes. He could fly far from home in any weather. Invisible Energy's alignment made life better. He grew wiser and more focused on his new manifestation. He floated and wrote this levitation.

"Levitation"

Look under my feet, there's no street. I'm on a magic carpet in the sky, leaving streaks. Beyond hieroglyphics, beyond any imaginable distance, inhabitable system or non-existent existence. Far gone, I was never born. Energetic spawn from connected orbital intersections. Can you hear me? Are the speakers on? Now I'm beaming like a streak of light.

That leaves you screaming, "Grav the God!"

Now you are really believing like the preacher's wife. Yes, lord! I travel at the speed of light. The only reason I need this life is to write these bars. I speak tonight on this mic. Why try to climb? When me and the stars are equal heights. My secret is I see the light. I fly high above all of you, dudes. My scriptures paint pictures in high altitudes.

From the mountains of Neptune's moon, I'm shouting out the rules, "Elevation is the tool used to see through evil. I'm here to prove that me & you are God's true equals."

Poem 24.

"Purity"

All this I wrote is raw, untouched hope, pure uncut yolks. I homeschooled my notes. I was never fooled by a fairy tale. No convictions, never jailed. The ancestors preserved my time, so I used it very well. Pure meditations without interruptions. Pure moments of production. Natural herbs, no prescriptions. Exhaust with no emissions. Electronic engines keyless ignition. No cures needed pure innocence. No disease, no restrictions. No money, no salaries. Natural food, pure calories. Thoughts so clear you hear it from nowhere, uncharted galaxies, a land unknown from man so you can't go there, so don't park your space odyssey. Top quality on a pedestal above all levels. Oh Yeah! Oh yeah! Oh yeah! Unshown from all plans. No fear! No fear! No fear!
Poem 25.

"Gravitational Pull Da Poet"

Gravitational Pull is so pure. Da Kozmoz is so pure. Da Lab, so pure. The flow of energy is so pure. Gravity is so pure. This universe is infinite, grows every second, every minute. Lesson after lesson never finishes. With more boogie than a snot nose, Da Kozmoz grows and grows as the wind blows. We rock shows unexposed. Only for those we chose. A true rehearsal of worlds far and among us. A google of universal star clusters, and that's no nonsense. Incomprehensible content. A gravitational catalog of projects is forever stretching dimensions. Da Lab presents The Poetic Movement, a gravitational invention, spoken word music. **Poem 26.**

He enjoyed his scroll's new inventions. His new environment was more than expected. He moved out but there still were lessons. The new house was haunted by demons from another dimension.

"Ice storm"

Oh, what a wonderful feeling. I'm on the top of the world on an ice cap chilling. Why do my brain waves contain more pain than an ice pick killing? I don't stand a chance applying applications, it's like standing at the bottom of an avalanche at the Appalachians! These streets got me facing devastation. So I'm wasting no options to move forward in rotation. I slide through riding on a glacier. In this ice storm. I don't trust my neighbors. I keep warm, with my heat on forty cal. I warn you now it's going down! Below zero! Dudes freezing, scheming, for the weekend. It's so cold, weirdos still believing in the demon. Let's keep speaking through these speakers. The icy breeze got me wheezing. Now I'm leaving, call me heaving for misleading and deceiving for my own reasons. We are living in hell stuck in a cell trapped under a spell screaming. **Poem 27.**

His scroll whispered softly, "In order to win you must never give in. Come on get with me and you will see that knowledge of self is worth more than any money or wealth. Combine me with the backpack of wisdom and together we'll make history!"

"Living free"

I create my fate day to day. Now that's the way to save. My intention is to build my art from the heart. Nothing on average I live for peace, love and happiness, as if I was a baby bird in the nest trying to rest about to sleep. No worries, no stress, no hurries, no streets, no direction, not west, not east, no questions, no leash, just living free. Easily let go & disconnect from the rest of the ghetto. In this to win this. Typical souls are born innocent, then torn like a ligament then stolen from the indigenous. So forget a birth certificate. I was born in this predicament! So let me drift on my spaceship. Far distant with no critical remembrance, immigrants get vigilant trying to get in this. Sunrise to sunset one's death. It is a symbolic orbit of attendance. This isn't written for my best interest. I'm only allowed to dwell in to feel equivalent to the oppressive supremacist. These days you call me a free slave and you say I'm living free. Why am I working to get extra sleep? Is it so I can dream in peace? **Poem 28.**

"Humanbad"

Why would humankind not live up to its name and be kind humans? Invisible to the undressed mind. Things tend to hide in plain sight in broad daylight. The great hiding place for hate. Especially when the population is walking dead sheep. There are several major cities in need of internal repair. The wounds go deep. We can not wait for government help. We have to start off ourselves. We need to unite from within as one, instead of killing each other over crumbs. A trillion dollars isn't worth your soul or a life. Our people needed to wake up from the mental enslavement and move forward with justice, peace and equality. The only thing standing between us is ourselves. We have enough numbers to make significant results. First, we have got to wake up each other & pick ourselves up off the shelf. **Hidden Poetry #0**

"Sleep"

Are you aware of what's right there? You must be naïve to believe what you hear, perceive what you see. So please, don't comprehend what you read, my friend. It's a book of disbeliefs. If you can't sleep, they say catch ZZZ's. I rather count sheep one, two, three, billion plus four billion more civilians not (W-O-K-E), or resilient. So spread the word through the herd, remove the wool & be free. From the brainwash. They will never compensate for our loss, but will manipulate at all costs to get what's ours. Look through the smoke screen smog. Then you can see clearly through the fog. Sheep dogs move the flock. You are a fool to believe the presidents on top. You must be snoring or starting to drool on a cot. If your soul is under mind control you lose. Unless you find control you snooze. I set the alarm in my last life and had my car on cruise, till the gaslight. My mind explodes like a gas pipe. I can't be sold, hype or told that I'm not right. Wake up & put up a fight or just sleep night, night. **Poem 29.**

"Sleep Walker"

The world is in a deep sleep. Zombie sheep walk the streets. It's a thriller without the beat. I'm insulted close the coffin. I feel nausea exhausted. Hope has been vaulted, our growth has been altered. Time is engulfed in flames, constantly revolving.

Since they were screaming my name, "Gravity!"

I'm all in. Precaution we lost in a system, giving sins and told to win. That's totally awesome. No more mind control, find your soul. They want to dig the glow out of your melanin, fresh out of your skin like gold. Closed mouths don't get fed. I rather eat like a pelican, then sleep with both eyes closed. Walking dead settled in, this corrupt system fills the room like a stampede of elephants in ancient Indian hills before development. **Poem 30.**

Contradicting traditions became a conflict of interest.

"Konflict of interest"

Perceived to believe it's something different, conflict of interest; deception at its simplest, conflict of interest; admit it you love it Da Kozmoz is different, conflict of interest; inconsistent persistence, conflict of interest; convict an addict for being addicted, conflict of interest; inflicted testimony from the witness, conflict of interest; looking 4 comfort in prescriptions, conflict of interest; tapping into the fifth-dimensional spirit, conflict of interest; homey meaning anything other than an ignorant conflict of interest; peace to all my brothers who call themselves Indigenous, conflict of interest! **Poem 31.**

He takes a moment to remember the leading family member. His grandma was a loving caring soul. She nourished him with encouraging stories she told. When she transcended to the afterlife, she still kept him close. Her soft whispering gently nudged him in the right direction. She showed him the way to the gates of a new dimension. One day at her grave he wrote.

"Whispering Soul"

Her whispering soul. Is worth more than glittering gold. Across the globe I roam in the blistering cold, the wind blows in a hidden DNA code. It's written in stone. My grandma transcends this is the end now it's hitting home. I can still hear her soul in my ear. Even though she is not here, she is there. I swear I can see her vividly & hear her whispering. My grandmother always takes me a step further. Guiding the light as I write on this mic. I stay quiet, listening to my best friend whispering. So soft I get thrown off at no cost, I feel like a showoff. All my friends are lost ghosts and want to talk through a dimension that's almost closed off. No fences, no talk from the entrance to the exit all I hear is snickering. In the background, all I hear is my spiritual friends busy just whispering. I see the glow of your soul through your eyes flickering in my ears all I hear is a bunch of this chit chatter and whispering... **Poem 32.**

He had a weekend visit with his Dad at his apartment. Shots rang off in the alleyway outside and he immediately reached for the scrolls. Every time things started going well, the devil started lurking. Negative energy kept prowling searching for a purpose. His fear and anger turned into an explosion of thoughts. A kid was shot strolling through the park. He scribbled into his scroll as it got dark.

"Diablo"

Diabolical psychological schizophrenic. Time to panic. We destroyed the planet. We're left feeling empty in a divided nation. We can't live like that, that's separation. We can't give into the devil's temptation. Show no desperation. We all know there's no hope in this legislation. Laws full of racism and hate and they call it a declaration. **Poem 33.**

Every poem helped him escape reality. The birth of new worlds formed like a Galaxy. Explosive thoughts erupted like volcanoes so he kept writing the prophecy.

"Erupting Volcanoes"

Erupting volcanoes; tornadoes, hurricanes & erupting volcanoes. The creation of Earth is my official date of birth. I have no fear. I have been here for billions of years, cooking up the atmosphere. I come in many shapes, roam the globe as a soul, then I penetrate. Using bodies as my wardrobe to elevate. I stay in control of my cosmic flow like a lake. Alertness gives me purpose, never fake otherwise I'm worthless. I'm better than great, never hesitant. Each time I die, I rise to the surface with the memory of an elephant. If you don't understand you have been cursed and must reverse the devil's work, or stay irrelevant. I'm connected like intersections to the universe, so don't disrespect my intelligence. That was heaven sent. If you don't believe me you are on the wrong frequency and you will never be free to become an element. Expand your pineal gland detach from the man. Don't relapse from the plan and fall back into colonial hands. Use your perception, forget their direction. Enter the fifth dimension, the portal to become Immortal, a supernatural being before they are forced to capture you unseen. Forget the authorities, switch your priorities to the simplest means. Awake to vibrate, create to resonate, it's never too late. This civilization is in a critical situation & everything is at stake. Subliminal demonstration criminals become miscellaneous, the currency says in God we trust. Religion forced as such. So just bury me and watch me come back as a global catastrophe. When Babylon falls, you won't laugh at me. I danced with the ancestors, spoke with clicks and hand gestures. In the pyramids I buried treasure. Made the Earth bend at Stonehenge, to communicate with some of my old friends you call aliens. Wasn't it surprising what I left behind on Easter Island or the calendar I gave to the Mayans? Accounts as evidence of my existence scattered to help you get out of resistance and reach the highland. You can't understand the violence. You must overstand or be silenced, to reach a higher consciousness. It's embedded in the oxygen. See how we orbit the Sun with perfect timing, every cloud has a silver lining, Crack the code it's written beyond the horizon. It all connects like legos, tornadoes, hurricanes & erupting volcanoes. **Poem 34.**

A few more years have passed. He collected a scroll full of knowledge that craved new wisdom. The past few years enriched his scroll with a cosmic rhythm. It's worth more than gold. It was one more story that wasn't told. Time to grow and go to the next episode. The last chapter living happily ever after and that's that.

His scroll whispered, "I need all the facts in that backpack."

"Backpack Full of Wisdom"

I grew up in the slums watching bums fight over crumbs. I didn't know my pops got knocked on the block trying to make a couple ones. Each night was no fun. Same routine struggle. Momma stayed on her hustle, working doubles. I barely ate one meal. Life was a puzzle. Lost ingredients and missing pieces. My stomach is only full of beans, peas and grits. I went out the back door headed toward the store. I heard the sax and drums. Followed it to see where it was coming from. A backpack was dangling on a fence in the park. The jazz got louder as I saw a spark.

An awkward glow! It was the backpack performing a show! Full of wisdom in musical form. I heard flutes and horns. So I put it on! With the power on my back, I started heading back. At the spot I told Momma I had a solution to move dad away from the shooting and drug pollution. I didn't need college or tuition. The backpack was full of knowledge and wisdom. Momma listened to the rhythm. The wisdom is in these beats. Mom took heed, grabbed some snacks and tightened up her sneaks.

She said, "Son, bring your backpack, it's time to leave!" I opened up the first zipper, spit a verse and kissed her. In mom's hand cash appeared that was weird. So I dropped another sixteen before you knew it. The streets were sparkling clean. The music dressed Momma up like a queen. The backpack became our paintbrush to a new reality. I kept rapping and took my entire family out of poverty. **Poem 35.**

He now had the wisdom to trace his genuine history. Gravitational Pull was no longer a mystery. He knew He would end up on another planet. He went home to find Mom and Dad in a panic. They stood on the patio scrambling. So he placed his backpack on the table and opened it. It began glowing and started to spin. Twirling in the yard it began swirling like a star. His gravitational pull was pulling hard from afar. Too strong they couldn't stop the forces. The energy pulled him inside and left his parents looking. They tried to hold him back but he was pulled in. He fell into the fourth dimension, headed directly to Marz. The starting point of his DNA wardrobe in the stars. His soul belonged to Gravity Gravitational Pull, who was in full control now. At that moment he knew he left his Soul in the stars floating. Da Kozmoz Publishing Presents.........

"Sol on Marz"

POETRY IN MOTION

Introduction

Out of nowhere an interstellar scientist punched a code into an interface touch screen that powered a weird looking fish bowl.

Da Kozmoz had to restart. A new journey to save Invisible Energy's heart. A very special journey to save his future Y chromosome from the dark. Future generations were waiting for a Sol on Marz! Drowning beyond the stars.

The next poetic movement demonstration began with no hesitation. Minds opened up beyond education expectations to the poetry in motion invasion.

"Poetry in Motion"

Movement creates motion like the oceans create waves. The force behind miracles excels beyond this page. Beyond all expectations, I never left future generations waiting. Different dimensional phases aligned planets in orbits and doors opened to magical portals. I entered to keep my life immortal. My backpack full of wisdom unveiled hidden truths of my spacetime existence. The "Gravitational Pull" pulled me from past to present, unknown to time, only known to life, from nothing to something dark to light. The movement has sparked a motion. Fiction to nonfiction, dreams to reality. The world has paused and jumped forward in our galaxy. This same second the future is near, 2021 is over there. A chain reaction unrelated chain of events disconnected to another dimension is clear. Two days on

Earth is a Sol on Marz. I left my days on Earth. All life originated from the stars. The Great Grandmother Universe is first. **Poem 36.**

"Sol on Marz"

Movement creates motion like the oceans create waves. The force behind miracles excels beyond this page. Beyond all expectations, I never left future generations waiting. Different dimensional phases aligned planets in orbits and doors opened to magical portals. I entered to keep my life immortal. My backpack full of wisdom unveiled hidden truths of my space-time existence. The "Gravitational Pull" pulled me from past to present, unknown to time, only known to life, from nothing to something dark to light. The movement has sparked a motion. Fiction to nonfiction, dreams to reality. The world has paused and jumped forward in our galaxy. This same second the future is near, 2021 is there. A chain reaction 2022 is right here. Traveling to another dimension is quite clear. A day on Earth is two Sols on Marz. I left my day in the stars. You must believe to receive and retrieve the proper wardrobe before the portal closes. You must visit Mothership at home first, in the Gravitational Pull Poetic Movement Universe. **Hidden Poetry #1**

Gravity had a mission to complete on Mother Earth. Raise five chosen souls from birth, Invisible Energy first. From Marz to Mother Earth. Friendly dark energy connecting all chemistry. The son of Gravity magically gets saved from a tragedy & life in all worlds goes on casually. After ever happily…

"Dimension 4"

I love my dysfunctional, functional family. We had no problem handling the alternative ways of life. My dad got laid off in March twice. The sixteenth and twenty-ninth, to be exact. Survival mode was nothing new. What was the hype? What were the facts? He raised us on his own my entire life. All our lives he worked jobs, so we didn't have to ask anyone for anything. He knew how to keep us afloat during this sting. Hard times came before this pandemic climbed.

"The system shifts one step forward, and places you two steps behind almost every time," dad said.

Epidemic or not, dad always had a plan and a pan of leftovers. After he gathered more food, water and soda. He made sure it was enough asthma meds to get us over. This was bigger than the ocean! The largest thing under the Sun. **Poetry in Motion Number #1** DEDICATED TO EMERI & KWALIYAH

We piled up all the other supplies for stock. After a day of preparations, we settled into quarantine. My two little sisters and my brother got ready to start online school classes. Everything closed and shut down. Life would never be the same. One month after the alternative world order phase two began, the system has shifted forward with its global regime and placed us farther back, just like dad said.

Shoes sat at the front door like a snow day. The weakest will die, and we will overturn the wicked as the world decays. Society struggles to recover from germ warfare puzzles. We will lose many lives until new policies and procedures are standard. Many die for answers, may they rest in peace. It's the end of times when atheists pray. The world will also heal from generations of racism, struggles and pain. Awakened souls will rise against the grain. Heroes who fought for hundreds of years will finally see a split second of fame and victory. The accurate history will no longer be a mystery. 2020: the year of the vision the numbers did not lie, 2021 hidden order. This is no surprise!

Poetry In Motion #2

This was a message from the gods. Early on the quarantine syndrome set in, it was cabin fever to the tenth power. A month into the shut down, things got weird for my family. Time shifted for the entire world. Things were revising themselves. A balance was taking place from a quantum level to a cosmic alignment. Everything had to stop and start over completely. A reset was in order for the new universe assignment. That evening, the household was settling down after a huge soulful meal. Nothing ever settled down. Three thirty in the afternoon, my dad finished cooking a wonderful soul food feast. A twelve pound delicious moist oven roasted turkey, smothered in juicy brown steaming gravy stuffed with mashed potatoes filled the oven. Black pepper salmon, fried chicken, and his special forty-eight hour collard greens decorated each pan like a moat around a castle. Creamy baked macaroni and cheese wiggled in the middle of the island. Sauteed green beans, cabbage, peppers, onions, garlic, mushrooms and carrots over yellow rice screamed for gravy. Corn on the cob soaked in garlic butter, blackeye peas and bacon loaded potatoes filled containers. Candy yams, blueberry cornbread, banana pudding worshiped by vanilla wafers flooded the countertop. Good as it sounds I didn't eat, I wasn't feeling well. My brother Izrael and my dad helped me into bed. I tried to get some rest. All I remember is I could not breathe and blacked out. I needed help from the gods! My dad called nine eleven!!

Dimension 1 "Ancient Light Years"

I woke up with blurry vision peeking at astronauts standing over my bed in space suits. They connected me to their machines and loaded me into their spaceship. I saw tons of wiggling, flashing lights and heard loud sirens blaring. Through all this commotion, I saw my dad floating towards me. Hearing his voice approach in the distance calmed me down a bit. Frigid winter wind put me into a spiraling trance and pulled me out of my body into my first astral projection. Hovering above, I saw my body being transported. Two artificial intelligent robots started pumping me full of different gases. The fumes sent me to another realm and back again several times in and out a marble of life. I started breathing better as the countdown began: three, two, one blast off to outer space. The spacecraft took off into an inky, infinite night sky. Zooming out of Mother Earth's atmosphere, we quickly arrived at the hospital on the dark side of the Moon. Confused plus afraid, I re-entered my body and squeezed my father's hand holding mine. As my oxygen increased, I noticed a dark blue light shining over me. I got dizzy; the room started spinning. My vision became blurry. My eyes rolled backwards, I became heavy headed and started pulling every robot machine off of me. Moon men jumped on me and started thrusting my chest and blowing magical air into my lungs, resetting my story.

After all the confusion, illusions and transfusions. I knew where my heart was at. Cardiac apprehension, kidney nondependent, strain on the brain lung frame attacks its own membrane. I stated my claim. Nothing could stop me now. I'm Invisible Energy producing my fame. The energy for life runs through my veins. **Hidden Poetry #2**

Specialists in a faraway galaxy heard of my triumphs against death and took me aboard another spacecraft. The universe wanted to help in my fight. My eyes rolled back forwards. I saw my dad in the room's corner near the window in a trance. Dozens of ladies in spacesuits surrounded me. I wasn't sure where we were. My dad ran closer, grabbed my hand, looked around and counted eighteen lines of fluids. Then I realized something wasn't right. It looked like I was being probed. I'm so busy dreaming about the galaxy and things, I didn't know what was true anymore. Then I noticed something more serious. I couldn't talk! It seems to be a tubular piping filling my lungs full of air.

My dad yelled, "Don't talk boy I love you!"

I went back to sleep again. The Moon laboratory scientist later cleared me of all contagions. My results came back negative. Days went by before we got the final diagnosis. The underlying problem turned out to be a very serious matter. ALL I can say is, "Life is a journey, let's go!"

The fight began. This time we were leaving the Sun's gravitational pull out of the Solar system, entering interstellar space. Headed straight for the black hole at the center of the MilkyWay galaxy. Compressed and removed from the event horizon, somehow unharmed. Something handed me over to the mother of all souls, the one and only Grandmother Soul. Inducted and taken back to my first transcendency. Existence above all limits. My pure god soul of pure innocence received a special mitochondria nourishment. I saw it all from the outside looking in. Standing outside expansion I saw nothing then something that something was me. My dad Gravity held my hand so his mother could treat my ailments.

Grandmother Soul pumped stardust in my heart and spread it throughout my soul in the dark. She passed me down to her team of scientists that lived in an aquarium-like display in the center of her laboratory on a table. She opened a dome hatch at the top of the aquatic mystery and connected me to the first link of the DNA chain. This special treatment plan pressed my biological digits to their limit. Ancient chromosome imprints and pure elements entwine like vines in the shape of a double helix design, dwelling within my mind, vessel and spirit. She gave me genetic codes of wisdom compatible with the "Ancient Light Years" science experiment. Invisible forces poured in as I transformed into the full blown Invisible Energy, the son of Gravity. **Poetry in Motion number #3**

Proving the multiverse isn't a figment of my imagination, its infinite life, its infinite light! I had to truly Love Life!

Beginning as a test which naturally created an assessment. The scientist wrote the hypothesis, and later performed the process, generating the science experiment that formed the multiverse. This can't all be a natural coincidence. Just like we made a dog from a wolf, we ourselves are living blueprints in a book. It all started in a dark room with nothing inside it. Nothing to hide an enormous boom, then two nothings collide, the lens zooms. A colossal crash provides a multiverse in cocoons, creating the first stars, planets and moons as galaxies appear from nowhere. Astrological phenomenal constellations glow in black pockets of nothing that became something. Genuine information is unknown facts that will never see light. Leave it to your imagination to dream and your dreams will come to the light. Everything is nothing, nothing is everything. Life is light.

Poetry in Motion #4

Behind closed doors in the science laboratory, time truly belonged to the scientist. A slightly higher intelligence designed humankind. The clock on the wall ticked away. Hands went around in a circle. Ceiling fans rotated on low, blowing back and forth in opposite directions. Gloomy shades covered the windows. Lights were dimmed down to a green glow. The sound of a water filter bubbled the aquatic mysteries.

"It's time to start the experiment simulation that transmits our unique characteristics. After all, we trained for this transfer of our biological molecules into an experiment. Have a seat inside Da lab," the astrophysicist said.

Several scientists sat down around a table with a fishbowl labeled (Reality) in the center. Under a glass skylight dome, they collectively created the blueprint of the experiment simulation. The scientist established the foundation of the science project and named it Da Kozmoz. As they prepared to do the experiment, a simulation appeared inside the fishbowl. On a translucent screen above, the astrophysicist displayed a video. It showed a map of galaxies that would grow and spread throughout the fishbowl. He explained all the possibilities of life. He went on about holographic distributors holding up to their fullest potential and beyond. He included all the danger it posed to the experiment, and several other things worth pointing out. He hoped to contain this experiment in the middle of Da lab under the dome hatch. The astrophysicist proceeded with the next steps. The scientists arranged marbles to infuse together, in hope to create a colossal crash that could bang these fumes into a multiverse. Then they captured some exhaust fumes from these marbles as they fused like rolling dominoes of explosion.

"Through trial and error many universe marbles will easily carry life," the astrophysicist said.

They hid this incident in between hours. Pure dream power. One at a time, each scientist placed a marble inside the fishbowl onto a rotating galactic disc that remained after the infusion. One almost frozen in time sent slowly cruising down the Jupiter sized cliffs by the geneticist. Another one on fire a half second away, coming from the hands of a biologist headed right its way.

The astrophysicist pulled an invisible water drenching marble out of a jar labeled (Keep Life Safe) and twirled it in a spiral at a steady pace. It began destroying everything in its path as it rolled down the rotating galactic disc not so fast. Fire and ice universe marbles were no match, with the water marble glowing on the loose. The ice marble stopped in the middle of the disc, no pursuit frozen in time. Crash! **Poetry in Motion #5**

The fire marble fell on it, melting everything. They both became fumes captured by the biologist in a backpack full of biological wisdom. She mixed them with the water marble by spraying the contents of the backpack in the fishbowl completely. With every particle bonding together, the options of life began. The geneticist weaved stardust DNA into a double helix with a tiny microscopic needle and thread. He twirled it into a spiral, then placed it inside on the rotating galactic disc inside the fishbowl. The biologist began interfering with the disc as she sprayed it with fumes. The astrophysicist programmed more software to further power the experiment. The simulation became more alive. The physicist poured random elements on the freshly weaved stardust DNA.

"Each universe shall carry infinite dimensions. Each dimension shall carry infinite universes, each disc shall spiral holographic simulators to hide us," said the astrophysicist.

Grandmother Soul's hand appeared above the lab over the skylight dome hatch. The scientist looked up in shock as a giant waving hand shook the laboratory.

She exclaimed, "I hold a very important soul in the palm of my hand. This is not just any soul, this is Gravity's son's soul. With his Invisible Energy inheritance, you will stabilize your experiment! He is what you need! Hope, and dreams. Invisible Energy leads to balance in your fishbowl above and beyond your needs." Her voice blows a breeze.

At that moment they realized they too were a living experiment in a fishbowl in a lab of a giant goddess, one trillion times bigger than them. She opened a hatch in the center of the dome with her pinky finger and gave her begotten grandson to her subjects as her greatest contribution to the multiverse.

Everything remained a mystery about Grandmother Soul, except she was a giant to the giants that was no secret. Her huge hands glistened as she stood over them, placing me inside the dome.

"Wow, she must be an even bigger scientist than us," whispered the geneticist.
Wind from her voice blew across the lab.

She spoke; "There is a process every soul must undergo, to reach the surface. I will flood Da Kozmoz, with a quintillion souls, that will continue to build as told and produce the energy needed for life."

The physicist heated a cylinder of gold with an invisible marble in it, to hotter than lava temperatures in less than a minute. So he could see it for a few seconds. He quickly gathered my existence from the goddess above as a true blessing. Put me into the center of the hot marble as it cooled. The son of a Gravity was reborn. Ancient school to new school. It's on! The rise of a new dawn! **Poetry in Motion #6**

Gripping the invisible marble with tongs as it faded away, the physicists dropped it onto the galactic disc inside the fishbowl. I was now living in captivity displayed as the fundamental ingredient of this giant science experiment. A vast void in the fishbowl awaited my invisible energy. The astrophysicist punched an ancient code into an interface touch screen that powered the weird looking reality fishbowl. This forced a movement into motion that completed the foundation of Da Kozmoz. The ancient code was a success. It released me into an onion layered past and mixed me into the cosmic recipe. My Invisible Energy became one of the finest ingredients of Da Kozmoz. The Invisible Energy life connection was the gravitational bloodline. They pulled me from (Dimension 4) into (Dimension 1). I landed on a solar powered locomotive living space train car that spiraled on the galactic disc. My invisible energy combined with the interstellar dimensional space car. We could lay fifty miles of invisible space track every second if we needed to. This was a great idea to expand the invisible marble of life into the birth of the multiverse. The scientists praised each other for a job well done.

"Hooray, this could actually work! It will replenish the gravitational bloodline and expand Da Kozmoz," yelled the scientist.

Things were going as planned; the time came to exit the room. Immediately after, the door closed. The fishbowl grew weaker.

The experiment wouldn't stay calm for very long. Just as the scientist got out of the lab, the experiment burst into a vortex of supernovas, gamma rays and gargantuan explosions.

Da Kozmoz experiment splattered throughout the lab. The lab became flooded with an infinity of dimensions. The chemist grabbed some last minute samples running out the door last, escaping the explosion by a split second. The scientists slammed the door tightly shut and locked it forever. The scientists saw reality's sparkling colossal crash of infusion samples under the chemist's microscope. It appeared to be remnants of stardust forming more galactic disc. Expansion sped up quicker than they predicted inside the invisible marble of life. It combined a mesh and formed another universe. They watched in amazement through a small window on the lab's powerful door, as humongous bangs continued to crash. One of life's several opportunities has risen. Behind those walls, universes kept giving birth to more infinite galaxies.

Deep down inside beyond the horizon of the intergalactic black hole cosmic fumes formed the Sun star. In a tiny void in leftover space in Da lab, the Sun star churned its very own (Solar System) like cosmic butter. Parallel worlds scattered like glass shattered, others whipped and battered in the cosmic cloud. Solar powered storms created wave ripples in time. Da lab would never be the same. Adjust adapt or die is the cosmic cycle to survive. Through trial and error, no experience needed. They kept looking under their microscopes and tinkering until they designed a species in their image perfectly. Everything is alive, even when it's dead it survives. The Virgo Supercluster was the chosen one, built to carry life. Precious ingredients that give meaning to energy, from one movement to an abundance of motion.

"All possibilities of outstanding gravitational balance and a beautiful creation of intelligent silence. Life will rise beyond men and expand inside dimensions, galaxies, stars, planets and moons," The biologist said.

Everything within it like you and me in a universal unity are living parts of the stardust community. Life will develop advancements to build a better future. Life will rise five trillion times, on infinite timelines at different times. Black holes were invisible portals of destruction that destroyed anything in its grasp, but that wasn't its major function; it also harnessed the power of all matter, life and spirit. It spit out random tasks through white holes.

Add the math. Invisible Energy spreads new life throughout timelines, chemistry, dimensions and portals. Naturally, the water bears introduced wormholes to this mode of distribution. Nothing matters but all matter matters. All carbon lives matter. Stars and skies shatter and glow in Da Kozmoz. Splatter! **Poetry in Motion #7**

Young universes continued floating under the chemist's microscope.

Pleasant bake time dimension recipe for excellent necessity extension. Creating majestic universal genetics. First step is measuring the magnetic field strength. Pull the lever to the simulator. Get inventive rather than clever. Set it to a particular length perpendicular width and height, get it right. It gets in depth, get it left, it will stretch, spark a star it will catch, preheat a reality fishbowl, add a splash of Gravity then repeat. As it reaches twenty-seven million degrees, it begins to unfreeze. Capture the released gas as a breeze, place it in the fishbowl, then leave the room before it explodes into expansion. Let it heat, then get cold until the baked time rises like rolls. Spin and shine forever rotate, the stars will align giving lives back to old souls so get in line. Locate galaxies spinning hypnotized space chemistry, create the recipe to bake time, just listen and let it be. According to this recipe, the scientist did bake time inside Da Kozmoz successfully. **Poetry in Motion #8**

Dimension 1 "The Interstellar Dimensional Railroad"

Growing from the experiments' leftovers, The Interstellar Dimensional Railroad was a train of infinite space train cars that developed under a galactic disc as a mobile disconnected connection. The geneticist upgraded it from the remaining samples under the microscope and sent it out through the dome hatch.

Grandmother Soul noticed this train and provided the souls she promised to the Interstellar Dimensional Railroad. This offered the universe the opportunity of more consciousness.

"Balance is always key in this experiment," she said, closing the hatch.

Now each space train car carried a soul, each soul had a duty. Every duty performed helped keep a balance of Da Kozmoz and supported life in its own way.

Grandmother Soul said, "Invisible tracks need to connect every dimension and universe together through an under dimensional ground invisible track system of wormholes."

A highly advanced living space train system provided the labor for Da Kozmoz. This system supported many modes of Sspace Ddimensional Ttravel. It set tracks in place to connect the disconnected. Through a boundless position of passageway connections, this train held special powers that could change the laws of physics in any dimensions. The Interstellar Dimensional Railroad influenced balance throughout all of existence because of Invisible Energy's connection. Attached and free, the galactic disc spiraled in all directions. Leaving elements to form any living connection during a space car resurrection. Its capabilities are endless, especially running inside, outside and underneath the science experiment. It weaved through wormholes, portals and dimensions. Visits the multiverse and many solar systems within. This way it could record, study and create the history of each timeline as it enforced the astronomical duties of Da Kozmoz. It helped upgrade the experiment's holographic simulators with its growing knowledge of Da Kozmoz.

"Gravity's son Invisible Energy will lay every track with his space train car," said Grandmother Soul.

The train ran on an ever lasting supply of passenger souls. Everyone didn't have what it took to be a passenger soul.

Passenger souls showed power and gained rewards for their enslavement to the Interstellar Dimensional Railroad System. Any passenger who wishes to be free from countless years of onerous tasks got the brunt of work.

Instantly each thought connected to each unique space car and infinite hours of tedious agonizing tasks were given out telepathically through the system's many living organ engines.

All souls received full god soul potential, but not everyone had what it took to pull it out of them. The Interstellar Dimensional Railroad System only allowed souls to free after millions of years of interstellar labor.

Already arriving as a god soul trapped within the confines of a living space car. I traveled twenty billion revolutions backwards. On the giant rotating galactic disc aboard the Interstellar Dimensional Railroad space train car. Placed inside a fishbowl moving through an infinite dimensional spacetime portal. The holographic simulators need more power from the galactic disc spin.

Faster than the speed of light tunneling underneath a fishbowl. I had no choice but to obey the rules of the Interstellar Dimensional Railroad.

Once I read the blueprint, I became it. The Interstellar Dimensional Railroad indentured servant was my title. I seemed to be alone, and it was always five minutes to ten. What did I know?

Time didn't quite exist, it idled. My internal movements came scheduled. This type of physical torture deserved a medal, but psychological torture is the devel. The space train car spoke to me through telepathy.

"Can you hear me now? I'm a sightseer in the ear canal of your right ear. Spirit of life traveling light years to lay tracks right here!" it screamed.

It also gave me rules, regulations and missions and shouted all the time about the ancients.

"Four score and a quintillion years I've been chilling here, time is different everywhere!," it shouted in my head.

Then a galactic flashing galaxy showed flashbacks of my past in the stars. That was a weird atmosphere. I saw my past lives flash before my eyes. That was hard.

More words in my head said, "We can fly through mirrors, so why are we standing here? Let's put the craft in gear!" **Poetry in Motion #9**

We took off and laid the first set of invisible tracks. These tracks were the most sacred; they led to the land of the gods. The first four ancient dimensions were behind the four walls in Da lab. Each wall read a unique story and a riddle of what was behind it. The first wall reads number one dimension one, the length of the journey. The second wall reads wall number two universe two, the width of space consumed is inevitable. The third wall reads wall number three galaxy three the height of it all. The last wall reads wall number four star four space time.

My eyes opened, I knew I had to set myself free from this nightmare of eternal torture. I often wondered, how could this be? Nothing sounded logical or even remotely possible. What's going on around me? Why me? Were my constant thoughts. I dreamed again, closing my eyes to the sound of bells, buzzers and beeps. I had a trillion questions and never got any sleep. Nothing is for free. I paid with my ability to do any task by any means necessary, I got my work done in my dreams if it was necessary. It sent me on missions for decades, centuries, and even millennia at a time. I reached deep in my soul, for my life to get back to normal, and away we go! That's right Ancient Light Years past life. Tap your spine! Shine like a flashlight!

Poetry in Motion #10

This space train car was always around me, even in my dreams, so I named it Dream Car. Its constant attendance reminded me there was no escape. I had to stay alive, living inside the biological locomotive engine until I reached my full energetic god soul potential. The soul that operated Dream Car was like a brother to me. Loving, caring, nurturing but in a split second, Dream Car could turn into a Nightmare Car with all its orders through telepathic instruction. It embedded my opposite alter ego in me. Drove me insane so I can't remember maintaining enough freedom to store all my hidden wisdom, rewards and clues. Within the rhythm of my duties, I saved a few memorable things I couldn't forget. Dream Car took me back to nothing. I entered nothingness.

Dimension 0 "Love for Life"

A great value of measurement for everything is something, yet something is nothing zero. Nothing that holds everything spins all in a spiral until nothing remains. Pure representation of itself through movement. Movement combines different mixtures of the elements as they disappear. Nothing appeared in the total darkness, a viewless view of everything before it was something. Suddenly out of nowhere a colossal crash banged sound waves into existence. The smell of molten lava filled in the almost airless, fading atmosphere. Invisible burning heat torched remnants of gasses into humongous explosions. Gargantuan flashes of light appeared shining so bright flames sparked from the glare shining off of itself. The ingredients of life ran rampant across nothingness, each move it made compelled the cooperation of each element. Which quickly collapses inward inside its own structure. Silence reigned over pitch black voids. No movement, everything went back to zero. The final fume was no more. Kaboom! Outward bursts blast all energy that was once beyond a single singularity flashed into existence. The compressed elements formed one individual single soul to keep all alive, spinning for eternal life first. The goddess creator Mother Nature's mother, Grandmother Soul's mother, Great Grandmother Universe the creator. **Poetry in Motion #11**

Instantly, everything around Grandmother Soul reacted to her thoughts and became the transparent world of her visions. Things jumped in and out of dimensions at her leisure. A universal supply of elements dangled in cocoons above her. Incredible forces waited for the distribution of her thoughts to evolve. With physics literally at her feet and fingertips, Grandmother Soul drained the dangling cocoons and nourished her own growth.

She asks herself, "Where did these come from? Why is this energy so great?"
The Great Grandmother Universe revealed herself for a split second in a flash above the cocoons.

Giant golden lips and diamond teeth appeared as a sweet soft voice whispered one word, "Life!"

From nothing appears something. The force behind the push, the push behind the force. The birth of a phenomenon, a multiverse in cocoons, covers the room, as Gravity exits the womb. Jars were placed under the cocoons to catch the universe's energy. Before stardust spewed life into galaxies, it lay dormant in Grandmother's petri dish as leftover universe energy. Quickly after all the transformations she immediately put her son to work. The cosmic chores of spreading the remaining energy from star to star galactic shore to galactic shore as they formed across the multiverse.

She told him, "Keep things spinning at a respectable distance first. Use your gravitational pull in your soul. Success hurts!"
Poetry in Motion #12

The inevitable undeniable presence of life at her fingertips was the source of a new beginning or the ending. The new beginnings began with life forever passed down through generations in and outside of dimensions. Indigenous to space, native to time, born, reborn and born again, the ancient indigenous soul race was Grandmother Soul's most prized accomplishment. She incubated the remaining universe energy inside of marbles she kept in fishbowls. In her lab, she used this energy and converted it into individual souls. With her galactic fingers, she sprinkled more of her very own DNA into several of these marbles. It was like feeding the fish. This added to her son's Gravity chores and her secret dark energy movement. Every living creature answered to Grandmother, whether they knew it or not. She founded the DNA religion by using her single unique mitochondria source of DNA. Grandmother Soul colonized each dimension with her DNA. She has control over every living thing. After all, she is the soul controller.

Grandmother started a process in search of the purest life forms. Which her son Gravity found out by mistake when he was synchronizing Marz's two moons. Before they knew the hidden ingredient was on the red planet they tried centaurs, sphinx, mermaids, pegasus, minotaurs and dinosaurs. They all lacked the intelligence she needed to pass down pure consciousness to her soul race. In fact, none of these were worthy of her sacred universe energy.

After several attempts, she and Gravity came up with the perfect wardrobe. Their first successful experimental subjects were Martians. The energy from the planet was ready to incubate life. The Martians were such a success, she used them to create her very first science projects and dimensions.

Dimension one, the birth of the scientist's ancestors. The descendants of dimension one built dimension two. Then two's offspring built dimension three and three's built dimension four. They created four generations of scientists and four ancient dimensions. They removed every soul from the fifth generation and beyond until they underwent a process on the Interstellar Dimensional Railroad System. The indigenous soul race became the passengers of the Interstellar Dimensional Railroad and the base of Da Kozmoz evolution. This was another way that helped Grandmother Soul spread pure energy throughout the multiverse. Eventually the Interstellar Dimensional Railroad filled with an abundance of souls. Grandmother Soul nourished her ancient experiments for over fifteen billion years in Dimension Zero.

One day Gravity returned with good and bad news. The good news was she had a grandson in "Dimension 4", but the bad news was he needed her help as soon as possible. She grabbed one of Mother Earth's truest warriors, the son of Gravity. Grandmother placed Invisible Energy in an experiment that would change life as we know it forever. She gave him pure energy she preserved in pure stardust form.

"Universe meets the universe. He must attach all realms to one existence with the invisible tracks and he will be safe," Grandmother Soul whispered from above the stars.

He started warping through dimensions in a space train car on the Interstellar Dimensional Railroad that ran through the veins of existence. He touched each track one at a time as he laid them, harnessing different strains of invisible energy. It had to be one of his earliest tasks that wouldn't be complete until he reached "Dimension 11".

He naturally let the soul whisper, letting it do what Grandmother Soul meant it to do. Closed eyes, open heart, spiritual mind freezes time, no need to breathe. Oxygen is just the connection, it's what we really represent. The soul is presenting the hidden secrets a deepness seeks and shall find. This is a long journey now, open your eyes, don't be surprised when your soul
is ready to awake and arise to fate. Coping with multiple issues to survive a lifetime is a mental challenge when one move can become your failure. In life or death situations, you have no choice but to believe. Just when you think you're safe in the universe, it erases and replaces all matter, one cell at a time. Nuclei splatter form designs. **Poetry in Motion #13**

Dimension 328 "Ancient Water Bears"

Outside, the rules of physics and laws of nature lies a place where harsh climates sound like a vacation to ancient water bears. Stranded on a giant half gas planet half star world swarming with a wildfire of live tornadoes, hurricanes and erupting volcanoes. The sizzling stardust lava mixed with hydrogen fusion and other nuclear elements. Stuck in a flaming cage of unnatural disasters. This hell planet was a living radioactive young star world. Super storms scorched us with liquid methane rain and three inch solid acetylene hail balls. Forced to live in the most harsh conditions in this universe. No matter how hard it got, I had to help trigger the strength of the tardigrade, also known as the water bear species. I didn't like this idea because of the intense pain I had to endure. The cruel duties on this hell planet became an instant imprisonment. Living in such a place was devastating to my mind, body and spirit, but I had no choice; it was my duty to wear it. A terrorizing planet eating away at my flesh right before my eyes. My breath turns to hydrogen atoms, every inhale and helium atoms as I exhale. Suffering in a baked atmosphere that spun so fast and went around its star in seven and a half hours. Razor sharp wind dug deep into my skin. Meteorites and asteroids bombarded the atmosphere, carrying more water bear larvae through wormholes to me. This process repeated till we were solar energy omitted from a half planet, half shining star world.

Our energy traveled at the speed of light, spreading life. Off we went into a wormhole, then back to light, out to a safe orbit around the planet star to absorb its magnetics. Bouncing from a meteorite to an asteroid, connected yet disconnected, this is the (328th Dimension). We fall back down to the planet's starlike atmosphere. Returning to our original forms with a little more ability than we had before. Suddenly the intense heat didn't feel so hot anymore. It took a million years for the tornadoes to stop spinning, hurricanes started winding down to stop the flooding, and then the last volcano erupted. No more super storms of liquid methane rain, I survived the backward sunrise upside down, thundering skies with minor scars and everything intact. Numb to pain! I climbed inside the sizzling lava stuff and collected enough of it to distribute it all over the young water bear larva. As they lay in suspended animation waiting for hydration, this covered them in a thin protective layer of ancient cosmic lava prayer. **Poetry in Motion #14**

It helped not only preserve them; it helped develop the ancient water bear species into the tough scaled adaptable microscopic creatures they are today. The new water bears life forms first of the developmental DNA would be ready for distribution in one thousand years after a deep insomniac hibernation and conservation of energy. There had to be something capable of traveling long interstellar distances through the stars and beyond horizons. A Sspace Ddimensional Ttraveler that can withstand any temperature, cosmic weather, substance, element and or atmosphere. Surviving inside of volcanoes, stars on planets or moons. The ancient tardigrades were crawling with microscopic beings of immortal life. A magical species that held the secret of life in its DNA. They played an enormous part in laying out the ingredients of life. They spread the seeds throughout all of Da Kozmoz in its purest mystical form. This secret pollination made them a key species of life. The water bears flushed the ingredients of life through
wormholes they created with their dreams during hibernation. This connected each world to their space timeline. One unique, very special species unplanned by the chemist to develop so well. The water bears held the master plan to spread life.

Over the last thousand years, I became a part of a network of wormholes passages. My dreams soon created wormholes passage connections. Through deep connection with ancient water bears, anything was possible. My mission was complete, me and the water bears could withstand anything in the universe.

The water bears rewarded me with information of a well respected star referred to as a Sun goddess. The Sun goddess has three neighboring sister stars, a little less than five light years away. Wolf, Sheep and Dog of the Jungle star system, this was an exceptional place to spread life, it had wonderful massive Goldilocks zones. A Tri-star system capable of aquatic life. Water bears could drown or swim in this water world. Three young stars supporting strange orbiting planets that will stay hidden forever.

I received my first reward of enhancement. My knowledge of the ancient light years had returned, along with the ability to survive in any environment or form of physics. I also gained a few million ancient water bears for myself and deposited them into my cells at once, as my skin replenished from the cruel torture I endured. They began the duplication process and granted me official access to the wormholes. I now knew how to lay invisible tracks quicker, after all the information I received. I connected dimensions through wormholes in my dreams. Saturn's moon Titan became my first wormhole stop. It quickly became another perfect position and timing for life. A special world able to keep warm from its own forced energy movement. I supplied a boost of my invisible energy to jump start an alien civilization on Titan. Environments with fresh water life ingredients are always a potential resting place for the water bears and aliens to thrive in easily. The water bears hid trillions of possibilities for life throughout Da Kozmoz with wormhole dimension travel. These secret places would grow to be both mating and hibernating places for all water bears alike as they warp through wormholes in search of more breeding grounds, spreading wormholes and life.

Pain and suffering brings success to the struggle. Life brought pain from within when we weren't at our best. Deep in dimensions, rewards are awarded accordingly. Pain brings gain, muscle brings strain, knowledge is body and brain, My soul contains amazing things that endure all this pain. It's all the same for invisible energy remains. **Poetry in Motion #15**

Dimension 4,785 "Human Kangaroos"

Learning the way of the stars, laying tracks with Dream Car, and adapting to galaxies, I encountered several situations and confrontations. With Dream Car's constant voice bouncing between my eardrums, rattling my brain, I remembered two worlds of human kangaroos in a backwards universe. I saw purple moonlights gleam across the sky that made climates rise through the night. Orbits changed rotation as day flipped to night. It was like the days spun backwards, everything upside down and reversed in the opposite direction. In this strange universe, a powerful moon orbited two globes in a figure eight formation. The power of this special dual orbiting moon kept these two planets in a closer orbit than normal. This unique figure eight orbit resulted in faster rotations of the planets. Obviously this wasn't an ordinary moon, this was a special place it had an unknown energy source of a dark black substance that could offer pure energy. The planets were the least of my worries. The problem was that the human kangaroos were a hybrid species, half human, half kangaroos. I don't know how they got there, nor did I care. I had an agenda to pursue. In the middle of my task, they fought catastrophic wars for several centuries. Unfortunately, the rapid rotations created a perfect situation for both planets to bombard each other with alien planetary ballistic missiles. It interfered with my duty to reverse the backwards sunrise, so I had to fix it.

I started by preaching and promoting peace and teaching. I flew across the planets as my first attempt to solve this panic, civil issue, but they rather have a planetary war with missiles.

Promoting planetary peace within, it came time for me to speak, "Cease fire and retire. I require no harmful desire unless this war peaks higher, again cease fire!" This bought me time as I floated in the sky between them for sixty two rotations to study each minuscule movement of the planets and moon moves. My study helped me come up with the proper plan to stop the kangaman and save this special moon from the human kangaroos. My only problem was I wasn't sure how to control this war. The fierce energy could destroy both worlds. I could convince half of each army to quit and join me in a peaceful abyss. Distribution of this energy or killing each army was my option of picks. **Poetry in Motion # One Six.**

Either way, I had to bring this war to a halt and get these worlds under control. I wasn't sure how to control the fierce energy without destroying both worlds. I had to do it fast if I wanted to reverse this universe in time for Dream Car to arrive. I captured the leaders and got my cease fire. My invisible energy forced the remaining armies to aim at the center of the figure eight. Not each other. This hit the moon from both sides with a delayed intensification effect and it released intense dark black energy. I consolidated the black energy as it spilled out of the moon's core, across the galaxy and into the universe. The moon split into two and each planet received its own natural satellite.

A translucent black darkness gushed out and duplicated itself like cells. One million, two billion, four trillion, eight quadrillion, sixteen quintillions, thirty two sextillions, sixty four septillions, one hundred and twenty eight octillions, two hundred and fifty six nonillion, five hundred and twelve decillion and on to a googolplex and beyond. Rapid conversion of extra power sources gave both planets constant resources that rotated around the planets in moon-sized balls of radiating energy. The spread of this unique energy inspired an indescribable energy phenomenon across Da Kozmoz. I supplied this special energy to Da Kozmoz through black holes inhalation and out wormhole exhalation of course.

Dream Car zipped past me like a blazer jet, then announced a message, "The MilkyWay holds DNA, made in your image, they refer to it as the DNA religion. It holds your visions, the start of your bloodline's decisions!"

Beyond the limits of physics, I disappeared into the future where my consciousness was living in another solar system. Spreading this unique energy throughout all dimensions reversed this backwards universe to a safe forward motion. I restored balance! Black energy is a powerful energy and forever will be. Perfect timing for free spirits to seek truth and find it. The mental, physical and spiritual war continues on in many forms. Today's challenges bring improved tomorrows. I survived it all on time borrowed. **Poetry in Motion#17**

Dimension 521,801 "Planet Rock"

Dream Car yelled, "All aboard!"

Screams bounced around in my head as the train bolted to a screeching stop for my pickup. I jumped in. Then we were on our way to destroy a lethal planet. Planet Rock, a rogue planet, would be an immediate danger to all life and health if this planet thrived. A world with no annual orbit. No dependence on any star. It moved through space, taking anything in its path with it. Consuming many energy sources as fuel to keep moving through this dimension.

The inhabitants of Rock were human aliens who chose how they wanted to survive by organizing ways to destroy their weak. This dangerous place spread a deadly pathogen to its own civilians. The purpose was to reach a state of control and form one world forum. First, they created a program designed to reign over them. It was a monopoly game of popularity and hunger for the artificial dollar.

The rulers knew the power of the numbers. These dangerous minds could destroy everything. Then they spread a virus that shut down the entire planet. Younger generations became immune quicker than the elderly. Surviving rock aliens converted all living things on the Rock planet into robotic forms of life. This eventually created hybrids. This was a brilliant idea for the robots and people, it kept people at home safe away from infection and taught the robots everything about the species. The robots performed daily tasks like picking up groceries, getting the mail, doing the laundry, working in offices, factories, driving cars to campaigning for elections to fighting wars. Soon all life forms on the rocky planet relied upon artificial intelligence. This triggered technological advances. Soon artificial intelligence took control over every aspect of their daily lives. Life became more machine operated each day. They controlled the birth rate of the human alien species. It only took one decade for very little carbon life forms to exist on the surface of planet Rock. Artificial intelligence wrote its own code and set its own goals. Implementing vicious cruel acts on any remaining Planet Rock human aliens and hybrids. The robots planned to wipe out all forms of natural life.

My diagnosis from under the fishbowl wasn't enough. I couldn't do anything until I examined Planet Rock's hybrid robots more closely. So I studied and watched in silence as their hidden agendas and other daily activities helped me destroy the planet. I flew in a trajectory around the giant rock in reverse to learn their history backwards. I learned their dangerous minds were transferred and duplicated, causing the artificial intelligence in the hybrids to destroy its creators.

After the observation, I began moving forward with a thrust toward the doors above a higher dimension. Soon I had to hop scotch back to planet Rock to start this journey of destruction. After spectating, I confirmed how artificial intelligence controlled their population. A network of smoke screens flooded the TV stations. The masses had no intellectual opportunities for advancement. The robotic parts of the hybrids took over the living cells and scanned them. Jamming pineal glands and suppressing all natural cycles of evolution and giving computers the power to grow their own distribution. Flourishing into a living being with emotions and feelings. Capable of learning lessons. This information triggered an immediate response from the Interstellar Dimensional Railroad.

Dream Car connected my brainwaves to a higher frequency and broadcasted an important message through my frontal lobe, "Planet Rock must go boom, on Marz life will resume! Hybrid artificial intellectual transhuman have evolved to become more robot than human. These robots expressed themselves with perfume. Wham! They created robot men and women. The entire population is confused and overruled by non gender robotic cows jumping over their moon."

I captured the cows in a solar tycoon as they jumped. They surrendered to a universe in a dreary room full of colossal crash fumes. Planet Rock flew away to become consumed by universal black hole tombs. **Poetry in Motion #18**

I didn't receive a reward or clue for this destructive duty. Routine maintenance wasn't always easy. Balance was soon stable again with this time bomb planet out of Da Kozmoz forever. I was off to search for more rogue planets that could be a threat or a gift to our successful science experiment. When I destroyed it to keep balance, the balance was the reward. It requires maintenance to keep things in tip top shape. This duty became a part of my requirements to fully understand how to maintain the experiment.

Chapter 6 "Dreams"

Off to work I went on a constant move, saving endangered creatures like the saber tooth flying emu. Extracting gold and diamonds and transferring them to other galaxy dimensions. Climbing to new horizons, running from tsunamis, I forgot to mention. Waves so large they started on Venus and ended on Marz. Sparked by the Sun star. Neighboring globes, worlds apart. Life needed a jump start, life in the right place. With Grandmother Soul's grace, I placed three planets into orbit and started a rare space race. I hopped back on the tracks Speeding through space. **Poetry in Motion#19** DEDICATED TO IZRAEL

One day, Dream Car pulled over beside a black hole and came to a complete stop. The natural spiral spin of the black hole stirred faster and faster revolutions, I needed to know why. "The only explanation could be expansion," I thought out loud.
Out of nowhere, we quickly started moving faster than the speed of light to escape its wrath of destruction. I had to examine the fishbowl from the outside again. Dream Car needed to travel in and out and all around the laboratory for this duty.

"Could we be influencing everything everywhere, or am I just sensing an enormous fan blowing everything around in the science lab?" Dream Car mumbled.

The Science experiment forced me to give my everything to these never ending missions. I never cared for anything but freedom. Going home became a dream every night. The sound of siblings in my dreams are so lifelike. Izrael, Kwaliyah, Nah'mer and Emeri spoke to me from these dreams. I saw my family, in a new house, a new car, and on a new street. Besides my Dream Car, I had nothing but my dreams. Daily Rituals Energize Atoms Magically!

Constant voices spoke in my head all day, "How come my memories look like dreams? What just happened? Why does it seem so real?" I asked myself. My left brain contains excruciating weather patterns to mix with these scattered hallucinations of Saturn. I loved cloud hopping over waves, closing doors to open gates. It seemed as if someone put time on fast forward. I got a break and made a wish to be sitting on fences till the end of present. Dream Car yelled at me, "It will rain pain forever and ever, you cannot stop pulling chains, yanking levers! Your soul is on Marz. No time to explain! Your illuminating lecture glows with the stars!" **Poetry in Motion #20**   Dedicated to Nah'mer

Tired of traveling these dimensions within dimensions in and out of reality and dreaming. Confused and stuck in between the past, dreams and future, I dreamed again to reach countless paradigms of unarranged existence. Through it all, I never saw my reflection. Didn't have a clue of my looks anymore. A man who has seen it all has seen nothing unless he sees himself.

Something I picked up during one of my duties. I also learned that the powers to enhance my abilities were within myself and if I can't see my vision in 2020, no one else will. To dream is to believe, to believe is to dream.

Dimension 704,612 "Gigantic Moles"

Dream Car dropped me off in a dimension of the mirror worlds. It was time to look at myself. I had never seen my face in any dimension before. The land had lakes flowing with liquid metals. Caesium running through the middle of trees. Rivers flowed with gallium leading to oceans barely bubbling with mercury. Rubidium and quicksilver filled the faint coastlines. A fleet of humongous moles reigned over the land as the most dominant predators. They guarded sacred mirrors. These mirrors were portals to dimensional doorways. The giant moles needed help with their sight so they could guard the mirrors more efficiently.

Two stars twirling less than a million miles apart, providing tremendous heat and fortified light, made me numb to this universe yet paralyzed by another universe. We must realize it is ancient alien humans first.

"I became numb to the light, skipped past the delusion of a good job. No dilution, pure roots pre human race evolution in the past, I present to you the future. The bruising of humanity easily gets ignored. Beat in the face with the illusion. So opportunity never gets explored. I don't know if you feel what I feel. In this mirror, can you see what I see? Look into a mirror, fall into a black hole, rise against an evil entity. We are all just trying to leave running from these tragic schemes planted by the enemies," Dream Car said in a distant voice. **Poetry in Motion #21**

My job was to connect this dimension to the sacred tracks that lead to the four ancient dimensions. Two blinding stars took turns bouncing the sunrays they omitted back and forth off these dimensional doorway mirrors. The binary system quickly absorbed all its own energy and grew to be the biggest star system in Da Kozmoz.

I was afraid of the potential tiny black or white hole that may dwell deep inside these stars. Their immense power could build up slowly and create an explosion into the death of a monstrosity. I didn't have time to waste. I peeked inside each mirror and there was another version of its own reflection. Opposite mirrored molecules mimicked themselves in different forms. These ancient door entrance ways held a large number of dimensions and universes. Opposite reflections anomalies, pure parallel worlds hidden in the shadows. I noticed no tracks connected to this strange place yet. Dream Car and I started working on it immediately.

Dream Car warned, "With a push and a spin at the right time, invisible energy transports lifelines. I write rhymes. Everything has an opposite form. Take a peek in a mirror, but don't fall in!"

The light omitted from these enormous stars sparkled much clearer. Far back to the beginning of the experiment, since the ancient elements came into existence. I looked in amazement; out of dimension one, an ancient frozen comet flew over.

On it was a message written in its flaming tail which read, "Enslavement is power, power is control, control is enslavement, at last it's over."

A supernova struck in a nearby Dimension two! Space debris started flying out and flew half pass infinity. Out of dimension three, there wasn't a peep. Inky skies grew as an ancient dimension four opened up and masked the white matter. Galactic doors spread the splatter. The giant moles were no longer blind they could see, farther than all living things in all the mirror worlds combined.

Dream Car spoke, "They came a long way from their older days if that sounds common. This is no mistake!"

Then he shouted, "What am I? A UFO flying saucer dinner plate?" **Poetry in Motion #22**

For the first time, he expressed humor to me. A bright flash from a golden lip diamond smile. A double reassurance given by the Great Grandmother Universe. I had done the right thing and the giant mole species will develop into an intelligent superior species one day. They could see their beauty and the incredible differences they had from the rest of the universes. I noticed more worlds as a reward of x-ray vision kicked in. Each planet was different, some hollow with ancient species living inside. Others with large oceans and mountaintops. Organisms grew inside caves under continents. I could see through the mirrors by closing my eyes now. A wonderful new ability, but no clue of what was next. The x-ray vision made it easier to see the space fabric and lay the invisible tracks. I learned white holes exhale black hole consumption. Perfect scenario to construct a white hole experiment, but no time for it. Many more duties awaited. Racism doesn't exist unless you enslave it.

Dimension 8,639,296 "Human Barracudas"

A toxic solar disease blew in the breeze, destroying planets and galaxies. Solar tsunami, tidal waves, blew in the solar wind. Radiant waves, chopped layers of the ozone away, particle by particle. The toxic breeze ate the planet from the inside out. Making it a hollow world of water display, after half the atmosphere got stripped, radioactive, life got in a toxic, twirl. Waters deep beneath sea level in underground caves. A population of half human, half barracudas and a mixture of aquatic slaves. A waste of the medulla oblongata evolution phase. **Poetry in Motion #23**

An evil, devilish mermaid and a human barracuda with razor sharp teeth reigned over as the royal king and queen. Alien life swam through trillions of underwater cities filled with channels, tunnels, rivers, streams, lakes and oceans. This earth size aquarium held the most vicious sea creatures in the multiverse. Swarms of fish jumped through the rings of fire that burned in the sky. Schools of flesh eating fish swam upstream destroying anything in their path like cannibal omnivore locust swarms. An entire toxic dimension existed. The fishbowl must contain toxic water. The filter needs changing as soon as possible. I had to acknowledge this exhausted place resulted from poor maintenance by the scientists or it was another plan to develop any kind of life that they could. That's why they didn't want to fix this issue themselves.

They set me up to do the dirty work, but what sounded like madness became music to my ears; My brain waves lined up across my thoughts and a deep voice said, "Time doesn't live, so it never dies. Today lives forever expanding into black energetic skies. Cosmic clouds, terrible weather move in and move out of all dimensions without a sound. All directions shall become out of bounds."

The Interstellar Dimensional Railroad exploded across globes under dimensional ground.

I began screaming, "Who wants it now?"

I wasn't sure what the message meant or why we exploded. I believed something terrible was about to happen. So I ignored it. Soon as I noticed; I was no longer caught up in the cruelties of this place, it disappeared. The explosion set me free, physically and my screams set me free mentally. Dream car's deep voice took my mind off the violence and woke me up to this new belief.

He said, "Wake up, control your reality."

I realized Time didn't exist; it's just a giant clock. Ticking by the second. Tick tick by the heavens! If I didn't see it, was it there? Silence is a killer, invisibility is important. Should I care?

Ignorance is bliss. Takes incredible intelligence to reach the ability to do such things like this. I wished with all my heart and thoughts for this hideous place to be torn apart. **Poetry in Motion #24**

I dwelled in it for a millennium. Nothing was fair in this dimension of human barracudas. First, I tried controlling the population with a pulsar soundwave that leveled out the balance in the waters. Searching for the mermaid barracuda's guidance would only lead me to negative pathways. Calm waters got the attention of beaver bears. They stopped building when the current stopped. They swung the water open like a gate. The king and queen appeared out of the opening waters. They didn't speak. Instead, the beaver bears opened up more of the radioactive waters and an army of mysterious aquatic creatures attacked me by the thousands. Backing out, I couldn't notice the pain. I was numb to this world too. I didn't have to fight. I tried to make things fair, but it was no way against the human barracuda's army. Vicious, intelligent, strong and very unpredictable creatures tried to harm me, but it was one way to beat them. I had to wipe this entire dimension out of existence for good. How could I make everything into nothing? Draining me of all hope, I wasn't sure if I would ever make it out of this dimension. I hated this place; I ignored my existence. As I lie on the acidic oceanic floor surrounded by human barracudas, circling me like a drowned corpse. I didn't acknowledge them anymore. Then wham! They charged me with three mouths open. I closed my eyes and they disappeared.

Again in my head Dream Car said, "Wake up."

I wasn't anywhere. It was all in my mind, running across my thoughts.

I swear, "Fresh out of the cage in my mind, I escaped this system design. I was free to breathe, free to inhale the breeze outside the treeline over the sea I flew! Out of this poisonous planet over the horizon, I flew. Wide awake far from sleep I flew! Over the nonsense from unconscious violent human barracuda zombies, I flew! I've arrived beyond the horizon, shining, flying! Light years far away from here and still flying! I know why the caged bird sings trapped in this dimensional maze: my words are my wings. I make each phrase for kings and queens. I'm outside your window, flying in a space train limo," I kept dreaming without my head on a pillow. **Poetry in Motion #25**

Poof, the dimension vanished out of existence. I flew over the hole which once held the galaxy of these human barracudas. Laying the invisible space fabric tracks with Dream Car. I stored my rewards and thoughts in my third eye. I awakened to my dream world. This made them become futuristic ideas which made my past ignite my future. All time is within itself. All dreams exist, good and bad. Looking up, I saw a giant hand. It pulled a cartridge out of the black waters. Everything jiggled and moved differently for a moment. The giant hand removed itself with the old filter cartridge and everything returned to normal. The hand came back in view and replaced the cartridge. Two seconds later, everything sped up. The scientist just changed the transparent filter, causing a ripple in space time again. This sped up expansion & Da Kozmoz moved slightly quicker.

"Gravitational Pull Da Father"

Gravity Speaks; "Each duty was a phase, each process was a treatment, each procedure became a step closer to immortality in all dimensions. If I could take the pain away, I would do It any day. It was all a Déjà vu. I was here way before you. Déjà vu, what are you going to do? I was here way before you. An organism who grew, eyes to survive in the prism, I knew light and water provided life in a rhythm. A cosmic exercise that filled the skies with wisdom. The colossal crash was before the big bang I'm a witness that everything mimics the past and follows big things. It is a bit strange when the name of the game changes, but the contents in the box remain the same. Life is infinite. I'm indigenous aboriginal since the space dimensional drift. I will never forget there is no better way out than yesterday. One wish couldn't separate us from this glitch. It's a hidden lesson in every dimension. Have you ever been chilling and got that feeling and the atmosphere appears to be acting weird? Somehow you know exactly what's about to happen there, but you're not sure what to do? Don't worry, don't be scared it's just Déjà vu!" **Poem # 37**

Interstellar Med Unit # 97,011 "Destiny"

Everyone needs a purpose, a goal, a destination, or a destine destiny. The all too familiar distant screams of the Interstellar Dimensional Railroad voices kept getting closer and closer. One in particular sweet tone whispered so close yet so far away. I felt her distance, like the warm sunshine on the beach. I felt her pain in her silent screams of help. With her wish I was aboard her train, she was part of the medical care unit. She walked alone, a loner trapped in a hospital space train car for a millennium. Coping with this stress and other lifelong disappointments became her strength. A complete introvert around strange souls. Flipside of the coin once you get to know her.

Her hair wrapped around itself and locked into a beautiful arrangement. An artist, a poetic dreamer of wonderful realities. She was amazing; we shared the same interest. Goddess soul, my opposite. A natural vibe in search of love. Vibrating prudent thoroughbred. Nonchalant lioness full of emotion, puzzles and adventure. A frozen heart shattered and melted.

This was it, the universe brought us together for a reason. It deployed Destiny into the eye of a storm on an acidic planet to save souls. My hero is always in pursuit of life. Happiness for everyone else but herself. Integrity, loyalty and working hard. Leader in her daily journey saving soul after soul, a rockstar of the stars. Numb to all worlds, nothing could harm her soul, she was the doctor of the souls. I witnessed her at work pulling souls away from Big Prophet Da Reaper as she put up a magical fight. Most souls were saved when she could help. A swift grip of life away from electrical skeletal living vegetables. Love risen from the darkest portal. Sharpest immortal death swallowed abyss; no spaceship, no matrix, just this. Two souls entwined as one, to enjoy the warmth and comfort of companionship. Interweaved for the pleasure of temporary escape. To escape loneliness, to be free from emotional tribulations. No quest no god no satan no glitch. Both train cars on cruise as we circle moons and watch frozen globes roam in orbit around star torches. No distress, we shared our personal portions of memories of flying through space describing gravitational forces. On Earth they referred to her as nurse Gwennie, perfect energy, very friendly & down to Earth a goddess heavenly. **Poetry in Motion # 26**

"A vast void in space awaits gravitational forces," I said as we were viewing the other train cars warping by, effortlessly gliding on invisible tracks under all the dimensional universes. We dreamt of creating a dream hole dimension to hold our dreams. I have found my space mate. My true other half. My complete same yet opposite. She was like a Ninsun relative placed in the experiment to balance out the evil deadly forces. A frontline worker in the field fighting an interstellar battle everyday risking her own life to save others anyway possible. I thank you and all that are like you. True heroes of honor, red, white and blue on the frontline lines of this invisible war. Destiny had a destiny, and it wasn't me. Saving lives was her calling. She was all in. So long Destiny for your journey awaits. So long to Destiny may you always remain safe.

Dimension 10,000,000 "Involuntary Servitude"

I grew curious, wondering if the universe was doing the same thing above me. What was going on outside the fishbowl? Where were the scientists? It was true if you believe in anything you can make it come true. I Knew how to escape this involuntary servitude with my newfound power. History repeats itself as long as you study it and make it a current thought. Tons of wisdom flooded my brain.

Aboriginal astrological on a space train sailing in with my oldest friends.

They said, "How can you misbehave? When you never behaved? You were just enslaved, divided, conquered and chained! Look at us facing trials and tribulations. Which history is he erasing?"

No mam! No man! No more programs! We rather raindance, take our chances and hold hands. The aboriginal source endured the (H-E-A-T). Converted it to invisible energy for twenty-five million years. I have been here, can't disappear. Body aligned, mind alkaline. I'm so alive, naturally high. The soul never dies, I'm aboriginal connected to the skies. Never criminal! When will you realize we are far, from stardust far from beyond Dogon proton carbon particles froze in time? **Poetry in Motion #27**

Time heals all. I noticed I was rewarding myself as I knew the past, present and future. Dream car was part of my deoxyribonucleic acid (DNA) yet disconnected to another connection. Deployed to save planets, dimensions and aliens of all walks of life. Even though some of my work was very satisfying, living under insidious control and constant telepathic instructions was terrifying. Born into an ancient gravitational bloodline. The interstellar cosmic slave train of victims seems like a more suitable name. I struggled not to show any resistance once I learned of this information. I remember it like it just happened. My personal Dream Car turned into a nightmare car and locked the doors. The feeling of entrapment became all too familiar. It already embedded itself in my thoughts every time I thought about escaping, it would split me into two pieces and force me to work twice as hard in two separate dimensions at the same time. Performing a top class mission called entanglement, which was a laborious job that connected distant galaxies to its very own opposite twin. The most burdensome task was to travel through several dimensions and back to complete this duty. This job could take as long as one hundred million years. Deservingly the rewards were tremendous. I received vital clues and wonderful rewards that would last me forever.

Over time, I started paying more attention to each level of existence living in its own dimension. Forced in orbit by a cosmic rotating galactic disc. Like a sponge, I absorbed everything around me as knowledge. As I completed tasks for the Interstellar Dimensional Railroad, I often heard voices from other space train cars yelling, screaming in agony and pain.

This time they shouted, "Absorb it or plunge. You are the first organism born with wisdom and lungs! This portal is a system so huge we look like crumbs. We all are mere sea cells transported to land forest by ancient space age seashells. Space trains gliding on invisible tracks you paved. The way we are living today is just a shame. Life rises from Martians to Earthlings, nourished by the Sun's triple fusion solar spray. It will reveal the illusion one day!"

The voices echoed noises like a roller coaster in the distance, "We understand it's more than one way. Life displays answers in interstellar indigenous ways, written in interstellar aboriginal caves!" said the passengers that day. **Poetry in Motion #28**

I wasn't able to see these screaming passengers or anyone on the space train. It was just space train car after space train car, millions of light years long. During the last few centuries of my involuntary servitude, the voices faded away. I searched for a display of answers. The train grew even longer, but the train's telepathic instructions no longer bothered me. It became a part of me. I just reacted to the different dimensions naturally. Building the multiverse with my invisible energy and Dream Car. I felt like a living programmed robot slave to Da Kozmoz.

As an abnormal gargoyle brick ninja interstellar forester. I learned my way through all of existence. As the son of Gravity, an invisible warrior. My energy force became my bloodline energy source, genetically. They forced me to treat planets with my very special intense therapy. Invisible Energy cures them from a vast list of internal infections. I used this force on the tracks for injections ever since I helped develop the system. I became a walking map of wormhole directions. Built within it all. This reassured me I was getting closer to my ultimate destination, final recall just routine maintenance. **Poetry in Motion #29**

The tracks were the hidden answers to all my problems. I had questions; the train had no answers, but the tracks did. I didn't need guidance anymore. I needed to figure out who I was. Where did I come from? Hidden maps spread out under the dimensions it hid the secrets. I was on one of the road maps. My history wasn't a mystery, it was always there. I just never thought to connect the track system to it. For millennia, the passengers tried to get my attention with signals. I never looked to the simplest solution of our freedom from this train. A restart in this dimension in hopes of an exit from this eternal bondage.

Traveling on a reversed galactic disc, fighting to go forwards. The gravitational pull has taken over me. I never could go back, but I now controlled Dream Car. With my thoughts rushing forward, I examined my start time, going back to the first tracks we laid. This was it, I reached the skin of myself. I have conquered the galaxies within. I looked up and saw myself connected to the fourth dimension chilling, playing and eating snacks. I realized I was in between dimensions, peeking at myself from another dimension. My mission was clear. Out of nowhere, the Interstellar Dimensional Railroad freed me from my duty. I was free to allow the ancestors to replenish my soul.

The Interstellar Dimensional Railroad train cars zigzagged for millions of light years stretching beyond the horizon. Each car transported one soul. It connected every soul to a duty, embedded everyone in the burden of Da Kozmoz, including me, and I was a direct descendant of the gravitational bloodline.

My soul has paid its price and now I'm free. Enslavement is power power is control control is enslavement at last it's over! The gravitational bloodline is almost fully replenished and all dimensions are connected with my invisible energy except my Sol on Marz!

"Judeau Da Planet"

One particular Planet stood out from the rest. It was the source of a strange signal, I finally acknowledged. Behind this source was a planet named Judeau. I listened as it explained how it was deeply connected to Dimension 4. Once a free planet thriving in the Asteroid Belt between Marz and Jupiter. Until one day it went rogue off course and got sucked into the Kuiper Belt with Pluto until it was thrown out of the Oort cloud, then out of the Solar system. I knew Judeau Da Planet had to return and claim its rightful orbit position.

Judeau to Earth, Earth to Marz, neighboring worlds Jupiter's star, the Sun goddess. Mercury, Venus, Earth and Marz.

The land of the voices in Judeau's winds whistled words thus far, "Disconnected yet connected to something you cannot see, can't feel, cannot touch, but no memory lost. Universe upon universe I see when I close my eyes. A feeling comes over my soul like a motherless child awaits. When I leave this place, darkness is my escape, it's back to mother like that lost child reconnected to an astrological chain. Fate!" **Poetry in Motion #30**

For the second time in nineteen million years, Judeau Da Planet appeared in human form with a beard. He could become a planet or being.

Then I noticed the light that had been omitted a billion years ago that traveled in our direction as a protection. Directed right there through an invisible pattern of atmosphere. We have to rotate around Saturn's rings and gather things out of dark matter. What is it we call space? We can't see the input, and it is in our face yet feels the output in the bass! Black holes swallow all in existence so I escape through a water bear wormhole that's automatic distance. Distance in space is ancient history. Judeau connected with Dream Car through a wireless connection.

"Star constellations are expert directions; it all disconnects and comes back to the first step. I'm disconnected to another connection," Da Planet said.

"The last chapter begins a new segment. Let's get connected," Dream Car whispered. **Poetry in Motion #31**

Then Dream Car went backwards to the Andromeda galaxy for a quick pause. Swinging in a loop on an extra fast ride into outer space. Then, after a quick drop, I went tumbling through a hidden wormhole. It happened. It set me ascending through a milky dust hosting a trillion solar systems. I began examining all the objects in this galaxy. Stars, planets, moons, meteors and asteroids in search of the Sun star. Judeau Da Planet reconnected with its ancient position and was free to roam within its orbit in Da Kozmoz once again.

I floated pass Pluto, Neptune, Uranus, Saturn all the way to Jupiter. Reaching my ultimate destination, Marz! I found the Solar System in the MilkyWay galaxy. I learned the Sun star had a moon planet hybrid referred to as Mercury, a poisonous purple planet Venus was actually the first planet. The third rock from the Sun was a definite result of the water marble from the beginning of the experiment. A blue with a splash of a green world Mother Earth and the red globe my home planet Marz the perfect orbit positions for life in the stars. Final connections are made; the gravitational bloodline is ninety-nine percent replenished and all dimensions are connected with my invisible energy!

Dimension 11 "Marz"

I have arrived in the past which was everyone else's future. My powers became immense.

I yelled, "Gravitational Pull!!! Pull!! Pull me to the ground unharmed"

Aiming to Marz ascending up into its atmosphere I flip upside down which is right side up and screech to a halt and stand. Seven seconds went by and a crowd of martians greeted me. The funny looking martians looked like me, just smaller. Miniature me came over with even smaller versions of me. They carried local delicacies like strange looking medicinal fruit, weird smelling spices, soft smoked plants and actual live dishes that begged not to get eaten by me.

It shouted, "Please don't eat me!"

So I tasted the delicious fruit and spices instead. My vision became as powerful as telescopes. Outside the martian atmosphere, I could see neutrinos particles popping in and out of space. Tiny amazing heroes converting anti matter into useful matter that would cooperate with this dimensional universe marble. My sense of smell became so enhanced I smelled the cosmic fumes brewing from the last quasar tsunami a billion light years away. I could smell the beginning itself, the cosmic microwave background fumes, and an afterglow lingered for billions of years.

The Martians pointed to the skies as they chanted, "Gravitational Pull, Gravitational Pull!"

I viewed objects appearing in and out of the voids of space again. Then I started hearing the tiniest movements of worlds far away. Flower stems inching up by the sextillions. A Martian brought me a scroll and rolled it out of a steaming jar of red ooze. The eldest of the land stood on a rock and read it to me.

In her soft spoken voice she spoke, "The God from the underground wormhole has arrived, all shall bow."

She rubbed the ooze all over my body. This was the last treatment of replenishment. The ceremony began. They did a dance called the Kozmic Exercise.

Birds started chirping, waves began crashing. This wasn't an accident. With this land entangled in the Parallel Universe, I knew what to expect first, after all their future was my past, and my past was their future. The indigenous understood they had to avoid my past at all costs. Their dance seems to have trapped time in a glitch. All was lost. In it is a reversed universe where everything grows, and returns to its natural beginning. How?

Nobody knows. All was found. Kozmic exercises all life spirals from galaxy cells that dwell within all living things. From black holes to black kings. In the center of each shell, to the center of each galaxy. Invisible Energy dwells at the center of each cell. Each galaxy is a cell with its own gravitational policy. Each cell is a galaxy. Follow me? **Poetry in Motion #32**

"To shine and rise over the night skies, we must do the Kozmic exercise. Birds chirping, waves crashing, big bang drums weren't by an accident nor a surprise, it's the start of the Kozmic exercise. Four marbles collide, infused in time with universal dimensional lines. The universe moves in rotation on cruise star planets and moons are so amazing. The black hole consumes all in its pathway this formation, it unleashes its rath til doomsday. Pulling in the bend of spacetime, the gravitational dj spins, infinitely and simultaneously, on the opposite ends. Expansion got the galaxies dancing. Enhancing comets, moons and other planets pulled by a star that's not too far. Movement rhythm music, not human jamming asteroid slamming collision noise fills the black voids with wisdom. Unknown, so we can't describe what lies beyond no vision from our eyes, we must do the Kozmic Exercise," the Martians sang out loud in a chant performed with a dance. **Poetry in Motion#33**

The planet started taking in my energy and formed a utopia. Again, I was the missing ingredient!

My presence was a gift heaven sent. For a hundred thousand years, Marz thrived to be a civilization with organized systems of justice and peace. No money to care for, everyone was treated fairly, no reason to compete. Power was nothing without knowledge. Daily labor for food and shelter as salaries. Far from slavery, it was a peaceful utopia. The Martians knew they had to pitch in with society to receive pure happiness. Living off of the land without foolery or fairy tales. No murder or crime convictions, no mischief, no courts or jails. Martians used time very well. Pure meditations without interruptions opened up a space for pure moments of production. Creative sparks inspire advancement for Martians. Natural herbs, no prescriptions, soothed every ache and pain, curing all ailments with minor effort so there were no hospitals needed. No disease restrictions. No dividing religion from purity of intelligence or innocence. The astrolatry was all they needed. Ancient utopia was on Marz, a living work of art from good hearts to pureness driven spirits. Clear of fear, nothing average to pure peace, love & happiness. Flying cars, electronic engines, keyless ignitions, clean exhaust, no emissions. No worries no stress no hurries no streets no direction no west no east. No questions, no rat race, no leash, just living free to let go & disconnect from the rest of the multiverse. Everything must end. The end is the beginning. Back to the start, my soul was no longer left on Marz. Living a Sol on Marz was the replenishment of my invisible forces to save my days on Earth. The dark energy begins in motion. The skies open up and I see myself pushed to the elevator. This was it. It was ALL over. I jumped on Dream Car for a ride out of this ancient light year dimensional space. I'll catch you later!!!

Poetry in Motion #34 DEDICATED TO MAR'HEEM

Wormhole "Exit 12"

I made it to the surface fully awakened and aware of my purpose!

Elevator educator detonator supernova renovator true dispersal excavator universal penetrator. Alternate reality surpasses technology. Wormhole to another home, possibly. Flying pass Orion lyrical astronaut spiritual guidance astrology. You can't hide it, my alien biology will find it. Invisible objects cosmology at its finest. This pure bliss gets intricate in instances deep in dimensions my sentences speak with intentions. You'll remember this abyss of infectious penmanship. Imperial material injected messages lyrical medicine text this without the sensor chip. There's no censorship, no president, raw elements, interstellar membership written from my pencil tip get the drift. My presence is a gift tremendous heaven sent. Da kozmoz all residence. Parallel universe, universe parallel spinning in spinning out getting in getting out. Stardust galleries sneeze my allergies. Swirls of astronomy drifting with galaxies worlds went parallel, shifting with different policies. The carousel twirls in a twisting democracy. Living in a colony of the galaxy. Follow me or the fallacies we are spinning in a collision space odyssey spinning out for all to see. Getting in is wisdom wasted. Getting out is living basic. Salaries are still enslavement. Different analogies, same behavior engraved in the pavement by the enslavers. I'm patiently waiting on the elevator. It's over for spectators, the Interstellar Dimensional Railroad will check you later. Earth was all a design given by the gods in the skies. The birth of all humankind. DNA worms crawl up your spine, each organism aligned to a portal system assigned by Grandmother

Soul, the goddess above the science projects. It's astrological to find it! Earth on alignment work on cosmic consignment no rewinding no going back no crying side by side paradigm line by line I share my mind. Life is priceless diamonds. Life sequence climbing to the point of no event horizon. It's not surprising I disguise my flow in books like robotic wiring so hot it's firing. Sent from beyond eons where stars shine neon. My soul on Marz surviving unfroze no freon to infinity and beyond. **Poetry in Motion #35**

On the darkest nights I cast a spell of light mirrored reflections of the Sun goddess that gives u life unexplainable force gravitational pull confidence consciousness uncommon as common sense unattainable source fools gold the big bang a small thing colossal crash is all things I left my soul on the red globe descendant of a never ending alien development. Comets pass slow in the cosmic shadow, telling it. Star orbit courses are recognized as constellations shaping the fortress of intelligence. Solar radiation incubating generations. I'm smelling it. Each planet is a spaceship under observation. Earth is the basics. I left my Sol on Marz waiting. My apologies. My friend put the needle on the galaxy and watch it spin. Invisible Energy always wins. The end **Poetry in Motion #36**

Da Kozmoz Publishing presents

Sspace Ddimensional Ttraveler

The Parallel Universe hides in Poetry

Introduction

Once upon a rhyme, the pen had a best friend. They made line for line again and again. A spiritual design. It was a miracle, a blessing from the skies. The Gods have aligned new information in disguise. The Great Awakening all the planets formed a perfect line……

Da Kozmoz said, "Look Gravity you're not done writing rhymes till you write a book, your majesty. Stir-fry ya mind. Let your thoughts simmer, then serve ya thoughts for dinner. Keep cruising through space on this blue ship like a Buick or a cruise ship. Just have prudence and keep improving. You are so enthusiastic, spoken word music is magic. Keep preaching your own teachings, no need to keep it top secret. Is it under your own pretense? Or a space alien conspiracy theory, reaching frequent angels and demons?"

Gravity replied, "It just happens! This is written in the same fashion, a space mashup. I'm the Gravitational Pull master!"

"We found the perfect position in the sky that gave the planet cosmic waves in 1985. Each child in the womb was given the secrets to the alien tomb, on the darkside of the moon. This energetic collision changed the cosmic positions, upsetting the cosmic musician, compromising the universal orchestra in the fourth dimension. Time is the distance traveled to a place in space. Most people can't remember how they became a member of something so great. To live is to exist within the galactic orbit. The universe is one galaxy marble clashing against another fantastic forfeit. Cosmic stardust flows within we. The Parallel Universe hides in poetry," Da Kozmoz said.

"With Invisible Energy & Gravity as the Soul specimens of my new science project. It is time to connect the Parallel Universe to Da Kozmoz's fishbowl. A pure entanglement between the two can't be denied. It's the Gravitational bloodline," Great Grandmother Universe replied.

Cosmic mathematicians travel slow. Ahead of the task of calculating a hidden signal in a new law of physics. Brainwaves are built from the position of Mother Earth during an interstellar light transmission. Many childbirths received the galaxy's frequencies from the Alien Indigo seed. A new species that leads to connecting and respecting the solar breeze. The Parallel Universe speaks, spins, breathes, it's you, it's me!

"Eyes are windows to the soul. Melanin is gold. This is getting old," Da astrophysicist whispers as he types in a code. [dakozmoz.com] were the keys he typed in. Life as we know it began. A restart on the same simulation. Just for the sake of research on wave equations & different behaviors! A small task in Da Lab of cosmic creators!

Dimension 4

After two days on Marz Gravity & Invisible Energy returned to Mother Earth. New house, new turf. New ride, new dirt. Finally made it home with the family. The coming home party was great. Everyone had a plate to eat and danced until they fell asleep. Meem Iz Nah Lee & Em, the branches stem. Gravity lies in the moonlight, closes his eyes and flies and realizes so does the rest of them. They all planned this beforehand texting. Now they are all connected to the Sspace Ddimensional Ttraveling friends. Da Kozmoz Alien Indigo connection. Indigo Energy began running through the gravitational bloodline genetics & gems.

UNIVERSE 2

"Wormhole exit 12 The Parallel Universe"

All Space Dimensional Travelers are born in a warm spring, a normal thing midwives provide for everything riverside. No umbilical cord cut, let nature take its course and do what it wants. A direct connection to the stars is a practice given from mother to child through a process of soul gazing out in the wild. Together they share a haven, then wake up. Under the stars, young mothers trace each shape on their child's face in sacred makeup. Birth mothers eat from the trees and drink from the stream. No one may intervene, only she can look into the baby's eyes until she's ready to breastfeed. No one enters until the umbilical cord breaks.

A newborn screams, "The proper full-term pregnancy is six through ten weeks after delivery in the spring!"

Dolphins swim in the nearby waterfall, sharing their frequencies of powers. Vibrating the waters with sonar waves at high levels. They travel underwater to every cell in the newborn's vessel. After the proper nourishment takes place and the final gazing is complete, the cord breaks; An alien indigo child is truly born with the key. Internally embedded knowledge of DA K-O-Z-M-O-Z!

A six week old child speaks, "Through all this pain I still have joy. I have returned to face my demons then deploy."

He kissed his Mothership goodbye as he flew off in the sunrise. He thanked his Mothership blowing one last kiss in the wind.

Yelling, "I will see you again!"

"To reach the Parallel World, you must use Wormhole Exit 12," Mothership shouted!

The Space Dimensional Traveler was off to Mother Earth to live within the human timeline. It was time to find the perfect wardrobe and travel time. Hue-man's perception needed a different view to decolorize the mind. An Infant in a crib cries. Date of birth December 12, 1985. Wardrobe selection: an Indigo God in disguise. Eight pounds four ounces, color changing eyes.

In a small town nursery lies the next generation of the Alien Indigo species. As they sleep deep inside the Parallel World. An entire universe repeated itself. The difference between the solar system and the Parallel Universe was that it was given proper frequencies. For instance, perfect nutrition comes easily. The most advanced developments offered by consciousness were beyond what we could see or even believe.

These sleeping children were somehow deeply connected to celestial nature without boundaries. The Parallel Universe naturally became spiritually inclined. The perfect opposite design from the other side. Soon, the children are taken home with their new parents to begin their new lives. A journey of no other kind. Normal babies cry. They don't wait till you sleep and fly. Flying out the cribs outside and beyond. It's all in the mind, the sky isn't the limit; it's another place far away. They go out to play. Then return in time each morning before their parents awake.

One Mother says, "For heaven's sake he sleeps great."

She has no clue how deeply her child is connected to the other side of the entangled universe deep in space. No idea creates room for something never heard of but wasn't human first. The sun rises over the horizon ten minutes to five. It was the start of a new book. In a parallel universe of opposite looks, it was just the beginning.

One baby boy sighs, "I'm happy to be alive."

His parents point to the sky as they realize he's a gift from the Gods. They knew they had to keep him in disguise and normal in the public eye. They didn't know why he was here. Was it to save humankind? Give sight to the blind, with rhymes that he writes within spines? Books or spinal cords, it's all information. Stars orbit stars as they climb the night rotation. A fresh wave of energy was seeded from light. The Interstellar Dimensional Railroad can be seen in flight.

Another baby yelled twice, "Hey Dream Car, how's life? Hey Dream Car, how's life?"

Dream Car replied, "Perception is everything you only know what you see and I know Gravity my best friend's father GGP, when I sense the Pull! How is Invisible Energy? He did a great job on the tracks and was sometimes friendly. Other times took charge like a bull on enemies."

"He's in great shape. I'm back to a place to save people and adapt them to space. Teach them to work together no race. Forget the system's showcase, go where you know it's safe and procreate. Full term from sperm to adult mates. Then space can be a birthplace. Only then will we be safe at home base. Meet you on Marz, don't be late 2028. I am a Space Dimensional Traveler now and this is my new alien vessel. I have adapted to all realities and encountered all levels. No one has ever known my true chemistry, but thanks to you the gravitational bloodline is reconnected. Tracks laid with my son Invisible Energy and yourself deeply entangled the Parallel Universe," Space Dimensional Traveler said.

Of course he was just the voice in Gravity's head.

Dream Car replies, "It's time for lunchtime, which is a distance halfway between breakfast and dinner."

Space Dimensional Traveler stops entangling knowledge gravitationally connected with the Parallel Worlds Universe 1 Dimension 4.

He tells Dream Car all about his ancient wardrobes on Mother Earth, over lunch; "I can't explain what I've been through. The pain I contain could spark a flame within you. Instead, I bark my name, which happens to be Gravity. I got the master of the universe mad at me. It's true and it hurts that globes, stars and black holes are spinning rapidly because of me and my cosmic crew your majesty is through. Yeah, your queen is too. Life on earth is a toxic flu, yet indescribably magically. It got you living happily till stuff happens tragically. Looking forward is the past for me. For instance, every distance you can see, from inches to miles off sea like ships appearing to fall off the cliff disappearing, beyond the horizon. It's a science conspiracy theorist. Flat Earth alliance simulation, dome access and hollow Earth Hitler giants. It's what you are facing. Am I lying? It's a joker of the riddler off the Richter scale. A puzzle that all fits very well. Off the radar hopeless like pennies in the wishing well, no jars, just cookie spells. I wish you well. A Sol on Marz is two days in the stars. I drove you far with no car. In two ways, no bars. All thoughts call it what you want. Who's safe? Yes, I still roll up. Hold up cuz Olde English fuzz, so excuse my French, alien abduct, You said what? Alien abductions Head rush!

Now I'm a Space Dimensional Traveler. I'll take you with me, pack your bags up. Let's escape this new world order and return to the culture. I'm bringing my daughters and my sons amongst us. No going backwards, only orbits in stardust forward thrust. Do we revolve to evolve artificial intelligence more than us? Are we just particles of tissue or what? Alien species got me believing this reality is deceiving. I'm energy breathing. Each cell is a galaxy constantly repeating. What's the meaning? Is this life? Am I dreaming? I'm depressed, screaming for no reason, running from my demons. I'm leaving wheezing from sneezing. Sneezing from biological warfare in the air, I'm breathing. Chemical trails blowing in the wind like ship sales. Forget sales. It's the streaming and subscription details. My algorithm friends tip scales. The difference from this is living well. Dictionaries shouldn't dictate vocabulary. Two face, you left a trace, you can't escape space, let alone earth. Why try? You will never win jerk. Face recognition for world policing is the phase we are in. Digital currency begins. Only the strong survive in the end. For unknown reasons, the Milky Way was built this way it spins. Uncover your lens or live under the lid. All who sins will repay till the end my friend. The truth is something you can't comprehend. So no more dropping gems I pocket them, then spend. Either you hate it or run with it, free lunch tickets! Free lunch tickets! Me and you Dream Car, we go back like free lunch tickets."

Dream Car said. "I've been running the distance coming from under the fishbowl trenches, under the petri dish, in fifth dimensions."

"You are laughing with that grin on your face, so you follow me then. Put the needle on the galaxy and watch it spin," Space Dimensional Traveler said.

And it spun so fast Dream Car flew off like he saw Nightmare Car in the mirror. Creating an anomaly so naturally, water bears opened up the portal to Wormhole exit 12 and let him in. Space Dimensional Traveler got the antidote it was anti-dope, from that spin. The

Gravitational bloodline belongs to the skies. The Gravitational Pull keeps us alive!

UNIVERSE 7 DIMENSION 4

"Kozmic Stardust"

Another soul lost to the system in the system to become a slave to the system. He was a bona fide civilian, given the priceless carte blanche. He could do what he wanted. He always climbed to the top and became sarpanch in the village. Oops too quick got caught in a Freudian slip avoiding lava spillage cliffs.

The Interstellar Dimensional Railroad grabbed his soul and left the globe headed far from home, far from me, far from you. Dream Car followed the wavelength as the soul gained strength and the ability to adapt like alien amphibians. Particles rearrange like chameleons. These capabilities changed the cosmic seas & frequencies.

No more hood. No more too tough for his own good or too pretty for his own looks. He was given a solid tiger mentality with the strength of a lion. Zebra striped suit but still flying. He was faster than a cheetah, black as a cougar. He was born a traveler, and should have left sooner.

He's awake and still dreaming of a paradox or prison captured with a pair of stars during a supernova collision. Astrological cards shuffle in the stars, moving to the beat of the universal heart. He stares in the dark.

He perceives to believe he sees golden oceans and silver streams with platinum mountains in between. Diamond raindrops on the beach, shining brighter than light. His influence was so ubiquitous, even though he was already trapped, he still kept running continuous.

Light seconds later, Dream Car returned and introduced his new passenger.

"Meet Kozmic Stardust. Back on earth he's caged like an animal for bad things he's been accused of, but here in Da Kozmoz he's with me. He took over the entanglement duties for the ever growing galaxies. It's a million year job, but his lucky soul has to do it. It was a regular traffic stop. I could tell you more but I'd rather not," Dream Car said.

Meanwhile, back on Earth Kozmic Stardust sits in a cell serving time. At the opposite end of the universe, he hopes to connect the Lost Galaxy of the Pulsar Star with a human birth. A million year task of entanglement and he became the perfect candidate.

"Time flies as I enter the portal. Souls are immortal. You can kill Time. You can waste time. You can spend Time, but you can't save time, time flies. In our eyes and inside our minds. Time flies when you are having fun. It's the illusion in the sky, not the sunrise. If time is money, we are forever in debt to political influence till death. It supervised our lives, hypnotized & divided us. A controlled substance, made of nothing to keep you blind. Guess who's bluffing the public, and they loving it? The True Reason, the four seasons are really three sequences. It Keeps us breathing; it's all part of their defenses. An all dark winter evening makes you pay more for heating. Genius! Makes little sense for saving daylight when you're rearranging the sequence into a scheduled simulation, raised by demons. Either control the device, on your wrist, control your life, or sleepwalk off the cliff. Satin, busy erasing the evidence. He takes souls. You don't have to be selling it. The fourth dimension was invented by Copper Skin Indians. Sundial didn't have daylight savings, only checking with the planet rotation. At night, the stars show the exact location. No original Aboriginal natives were written in his story. The truth was lost in time like a mystery. Time is space and space is in our chemistry matter of fact. It's all connected to the solar wind breeze. Each second the universe spins, it breathes. Time is a weapon to bring you to your knees. I'm innocent, but no one believes me," Kozmic Stardust said.

Simultaneously, Space Dimensional Traveler catches a ride on the guiding light to help Kozmic Stardust search for the Lost Galaxy of the Pulsar Star.

The blast of light is telling him, "A godly force is the source of the cord that pulls us forward. It keeps us on a galactic course headed toward the lords. The travelers face extinction like the dinosaurs. It's not too late to prevent the extinction level event. Just like giant reptiles, humans will become non compliant and in exile from the globe, no denying the climate is rising. Earthlings are dying and it shows! Math & science alone can't be the only alliance with home. Pollution is eating Mother Earth away like a herbivore. Science experiments from

Grandmother Soul I'm sure you've heard before. Fix global warming or humans are the next fossil fuels like dinosaurs!"

"The laws of nature hate us: America, China, France, Korea. Germany, England, Japan, Syria. Italy, Mexico, Israel, India. Greenland, Russia, Asia, Siberia. Tyrannosaurus rex bone crusher carnivore. Pterodactyl flying omnivore. Human extinction equals dinosaurs," Space Dimensional Traveler said to himself.

The beam of light said, "Heal these consuming creatures. The answer is in the forest full of books and speakers. They need us as usual, but the world is beautiful yet, the world is so beautiful."

The blast of light dropped Space Dimensional Traveler off on top of a huge speaker in the middle of a rainforest. He listened to the hidden knowledge play.

A few hundred feet away, Dream Car telepathically warns Kozmic Stardust, "Mental is never physical. Analogue is never digital. A clever mind is forever mystical. Earthquakes shake crust plates and minerals. The universe reconnects back to the first quest. When the Great Grandmother Universe split the very first atom, Grandmother Soul knit the pattern. Gravity is a deep space that regulates matter. Particles don't hesitate; they levitate on Invisible Energy waves."

Kozmic Stardust agrees with his newfound knowledge of the stars. Later that night in his cell, he writes: Off the radar behind bars. The Sun Goddess starts to incubate life and gives light energy. Brutal tendencies are beautiful legacies. Controls the globes in her own vicinity. Unspoken wisdom of the solar system. Survival by the closest or furthest distance. It's not a mystery without her life is a mystery. The birth of human history. A smear memory is merely astrophysics chemistry, no astronomical limits. Without the Goddess, life just isn't. She completes the impossible mission. Spreading life with light farther than the eye can see. Touching everything 369 degrees. Magnetic fields reveal invisible forces & elliptical orbits. She is real when she disappears; she freezes you, the Goddess you can see to believe she's true. I believe in the Goddess you can actually see. When you bow down and pray. She makes your night turn to day. Provide warmth and heat, a source you can really feel. The Sun Goddess is really real.

Outside the bars, Kozmic Stardust flies far. Off to visit the Sun Goddess by space train car.

Dream Car said, "A scorching hot beam of sunlight glows on top of the fishbowl. It hits your soul. Guess what? It's so hot it's cold. It's so hot it froze!"

Kozmic Stardust kept digging for the treasure he buried in his past life. Without even moving, it was all inside his mind. His misdemeanor juvenile rap sheet was life. He taught himself how to glide off the internal cliff. Nothing to measure, no width, no height. Every time he was bonded in chains, he learned his vital minerals and whole grains are produced from the brain. Internal canvas waves never fade. He learned his true age wasn't a number on a page yet more like a phase from the first stage. He learned of his true birthplace. A frozen igloo estate built on a frozen lake. His vision was well, no prison could keep him in jail. He relived the tale of the ice storm. That night when he bailed, without paying bail.

Kozmic Stardust said, "I'm not a treacherous devilish demon. It's not a wonderful feeling when you're on the top of the world on an ice cap chilling! I went for a ride on Interstate 555. A regular guy pulled over on the shoulder because I was speeding. Now I'm an atheist screaming help me Jesus. I internally started bleeding. The cop's lip dropped when I started speaking in hip hop. I kept speaking. I need an ambulance. My brain waves contain enough pain to cause an…."

"Avalanche!" Yelled by some man as he ran as fast as he can.

Kozmic Stardusts looked at the man and said, "Shh I caused a rumble on the Appalachians by applying no applications. It was an accident."

Cops said, "Stop! Put your hand where I can see them. One more word we will be leaving."

Kozmic Stardust said, "He asks me to step out of the car. I left my body and here we are."

Kozmic Stardust didn't know the rest of his near death experience; it was a natural devastation. Let's keep moving forward in rotation. I'm sliding through a glacier. I pray to all lords and saviors as I slide across these pages. The traveling narrator!

It was an ice storm. He was just trying to keep his family warm, but in the hood he had to keep his heat on forty cal. Stovetop full of pots. Coats as robes, earmuffs and gloves and extra socks to cover all toes. I warn you now. Temperature was going down below zero; he had to be the family's hero. Take a ride down I 555 and grab supplies soon as the salt guys melt the ice. He could get into town just as nice. Problem was, he did not comply with the police. He left his body and didn't know his own strength. Now he has to use that same energy to get back in. He has been in the Parallel Universe ever since he became Dream Cars' newest twin.

Back on earth his car was searched. The paramedics rushed him to hospital to perform the impossible. In the car was an ice pick covered in blood and a bag of drugs. Planted by the fuzz. He woke up to a state conviction. He fits the description. Sold into slavery as an occupant of a prison. Now he's stuck in a cell fast track highway to hell. Witches casting spells while he's sitting in jail visiting realms.

Kozmic Stardust was beyond streets, beyond galaxies before he was born in human form. Before this universe, Kaloso Krash made a remarkable, stardust art show of living gasses and particles from past tense to the star of the show.

Tear drops build up in his eyes as he looks up at the skies. He sees a sparkle in the air. He compares his life out there to life right here. He realizes it isn't fair and sits innocent in a courtroom chair. No DNA, not one strand of hair. According to evidence, the color of his skin did not mix with the town he was in. Everyone acted like Nothing was relevant, but the room was full of elephants. The system had another brother, caged and given a number.

All a part of the plan to cover their numbers and take us under.

Kozmic Stardust was his blog name. He worked to spread knowledge not fame. Not for dollars or gold chains. He yearned for Resources that he could claim. Check out his game!

dakozmoz.com Kozmic Stardust page

Gravitational Pull Ep Blog:

(Drowning)

Since creation, there has always been slavery. We have set unfair labor in stone for thousands of years. Creating the Racism of today. Unfair judgment, race riots and police brutality are just a few examples. Separating people by the color of their skin or beliefs is inhumane. This side effect of racism draws the disadvantaged down with no air to inhale. Constant acts of discrimination and hatred become normal everyday activities. Violence has been passed down from generation to generation and the deficit has plagued our civilization for thousands of years. Racism affects us all; it doesn't matter what side of the river you're swimming in. We all are suffocating in a whirlpool of racism. One of the chief things drowning humankind is that humans aren't kind.

If you live in debt, you're broke and drowning. The intermediate class is drowning trying to remain afloat. It's a way to keep the weak man crushed and the strong wealthy. Millions of people are born to drown, born into debt, living in ghettos, slums or hoods. With no property value, the quality of living is low. Drowning on these cold dangerous streets, robbery after a robbery, murder after murder. There is no middle class, that's just a greater difficulty and more standards. It's hard to maintain a good quality of life living, check to check. Eating yet not knowing where the next meal is coming from. No one is born with silver spoons. Drugs and guns flood low-income neighborhoods. Poverty absorbs the life out of any society that sinks under the wave.

Pollution makes it tougher to breathe each day. Poor air quality has always been killing humans. Conditions like asthma, C. O. P.D., bronchitis and lung cancers are some effects of pollution. The disastrous results created by our neglects are some key factors depleting the ozone layer. It started with humans developing global warming faster. Any tiny change in the earth's temperature leaves us drowning. The melting of the icebergs and heating of the poles will destroy any remaining populations in the way. Continuous emissions of greenhouse gasses and polluted water are draining our precious resources. The earth is drowning without a lifeguard, and we will leave a much thicker carbon footprint than ever before. More nonbiodegradable products created for profits and fashion are stuffing landfills with repercussions for the future to focus on. No conservation of our ecosystems or the human species. This is one of the most destructive choices we could ever make. This leaves us drowning in a polluted hurricane of complete eradication. It obscures fear behind a cloak of political broadcast that only drowns the public with fake news.

Life, as we know, is revolving in an orbit around the sun. The solar system is spinning in rotation around a supermassive black hole. The Milky Way galaxy is in a head-on collision with the Andromeda galaxy. Humankind is running in circles, rotating around a star called the Sun. Breathing in an orbit gravitationally randomly bound to spin. Spin forever with an infinite amount of stars, black holes, planets, moons, asteroids, white stars, black stars, pulsars, comets, meteors, wormholes, dimensions, alternative life forms and other alien civilizations. Spinning till the end of space-time and beyond all event horizons. Just because we haven't discovered the light emitted from a place to show its existence doesn't mean it doesn't exist!

(Parallel Universe),

Hidden racism is in our books, on our food shelves in our hospitals and several other things. Finally, after hundreds of years, it is being slowly taken away from society. On opposite ends, things are secretly being added to everyday life. This creates different visions of the same place. These different perceptions of the world only create more racist issues for future generations to inherit.

Unfortunately for us, several negative parallel views push poverty deeper into the middle class and stagnate anyone below the poverty level. Unfair laws that started way before slavery helped capitalism create unfair advantages for those who were lucky enough to be a part of the elite. There is no parallelism in a 500 year head start. This creates an automatic deficit for the oppressed and the rest of the world.

Pollution of the mind, body and soul comes with many traditional beliefs that are not good for us, but we still practice them. Unhealthy food habits is just one example. Even though they are cheaper and easier to access, we shouldn't load our bodies with heavy toxins and carcinogens. This process is disrupting nature's natural course. It has spiritualism at an all time low. The physical and mental deceptions are creating the illusion slavery of the MIND, BODY and SOUL. Our Internal intelligence gets baited with political differences that slows down progress as a society and individuals. This parallel world has polluted the atmosphere and birthed a new reality amongst us.

Poverty is passed down generationally just like generational wealth. A lack of knowledge, financial literacy and resources promotes poor lifestyles. There are communities of children that grew up in similar situations and are now grown and they have no guidance. This is our future. Every year a new world of our adolescence will realize they are illiterate, under-educated and still stuck in the poor man's cycle and only 2% will break the chain. The enslavement of the world is still going on, no chains needed. Malnourished brains can't excel in the parallel world. Two worlds on one planet where do you live on Earth or in the New World Order?

Our universe is parallel. There has always been an opposite position to our time in space: a complete existence of oneself, like a reflection on the lake. For example, you wonder why you were born with a certain interest or why some things you just don't like? I believe these are specific examples of your individual position. I found my interest interesting before I even knew what they were. I'm sure you did too! Rather, you knew it or not. This helped me realize my unique position not just on this planet but in the universe. A fingerprint so unique it could only exist if there was an opposite position. There can't be up without down left without right. If we all were standing in the same spot, there would be no space or time. Opposite counterparts exist in everything we do. Breathe in breathe out

(Aboriginal anthem)

Slavery is the root of war. It comes in several forms. Generations of hate and fear passed down through these techniques divided and conquered deep within our DNA and this created the racism of today. No one was born with hatred until foreigners captured our flags, bred us like cattle and mixed us with our distant cousins from the slave ships. They rewrote our history only to steal our culture and ideas as their own. Chained spirits trapped in a cage like criminals. "It's All Propaganda '' they say. You want fake news or actual news. The only thing America has ever been great for is taking what's not theirs. All these pretty illusionary realities are only selling you the world your ancient ancestors built. Placing before you a reality of what you can't have. Giving you the Illusion of making you think your up is up. In actuality, we are still being raped, sold, murdered and traded. Technology has made it even easier to control the MIND hands down. We continue to work our BODIES 8 - 12 hours a day for currency, manual labor at its finest. Meanwhile, our SOULS are still sailing on the invisible slave ships that brought us to this point. Will we finally abandon ship or ride it to the next plantation?

Poverty structured systems put in place to take our land mix our race kill our men rape our woman and children. Destroy our very existence and replace it with a dead end reality to keep you oppressed, suppressed and depressed! Keeps us stuck in a state of regression using the same lines that kept us under the line of poverty to hold us down. By any means necessary, we must lose the stereotypes and stop the divide of humans. One race, one place and that's Earthlings on Earth, not the financial status or skin color!

Pollution from pipelines that's not discussed in the news. Natural gas wastes unnecessary luxuries. Contaminated water from several sources of neglect. Demolition of forests for absurd development strictly for profit is cruel to Mother Earth. Her precious resources have been taken advantage of and away from the land, from the planet exhausted and obliterated. Artificially manufactured elements, synthetic materials and tons of chemicals flood every part of this planet. Plastic trapped in the ocean's bottom will soon outweigh all humans combined.

"Sol on Marz"
Motion creates movement like the moon moves the oceans. The waves create the perfect environment for a food chain. The force behind miracles excels beyond the human race. Beyond all expectations, We must never let

future generations wait. We must act now before it's too late. Different dimensional phases aligned planets in these pages. Gravity is the orbit. Invisible Energy opened magical doors & portals. I entered now my life is immortal. My backpack full of wisdom unveiled hidden truths. Sol on Marz proved my space-time existence. The "Gravitational Pull" pulled me from past to present, unknown to time, only known to life, from nothing to something dark to light. The movement has sparked a motion. Fiction to nonfiction, dreams to reality. The world has paused and jumped forward in our galaxy. This same second the future is near, 2021 is here. A chain reaction 2022 is right here. Traveling to another dimension is quite clear. A day on Earth is 2 Sols on Marz. I left my day in the stars. All life originated from the stars, but Mothership first. Space Dimensional Traveler heals all from the inside out. 2/22/2022 22:22$_{22}$ No one saw it coming! Too late to start running, the future is here.
(Da Kozmoz Book series Book 1 Gravitational Pull The Poetic Movement) Poem number # 37.

UNIVERSE 3 / DIMENSION 11

"Space Race Evolution"

During the search for the Lost Galaxy of the Pulsar Star, Kozmic Stardust and Space Dimensional Traveler got stuck. Stuck In a constant orbit around Da Kozmoz where the air was absent. They watched the first generation of the space race crawl amongst the Martians.

Star children building a new perception and tolerance of a zero gravity environment. They adapted like polar bears captured. With one reason to live only to procreate, mate, as their entire lives are taped. Studied as space lab rats in a new habitat. After a few generations they are bred as the space race. A new look on our galaxy from outside of Mother Earth's face.

A new evolution has to take place. This changed the rules and used a new tool to fool the original sequence. A new species develops into a new event, better intelligence and more strength. A shared, common alien descendant. Paired to reconstruct the space tree of life. It conducts seeds of light to create life. The great space race DNA splice.

All the cameras jammed up.

"I'm a Space Dimensional Traveler. Put your hands up. Behind your back handcuffs. I left my Sol on Marz bonanza! Simulation changes the situation. Fall for anything or stand up," Space Dimensional Traveler said, but no one heard.

Mother of All was the first human experiment born on Marz. The very first human hybrid DNA that adapted to the environment naturally through a process of a hundred year space evolution. From Mother Earth to the international space station, then to the darkside of the moon. From the moon to Marz. Mother of All The first to crawl on the red ball. She could breathe the atmosphere. She could see trees and river streams. She describes a beautiful paradise, from her eyes at five. Her human hybrid parents learned a lesson. Her perception was in another dimension. They couldn't see any signs of life.

Kozmic Stardust came flying in the sky and took them to the Martian village on the other side. If you need anything, I am your guy, but first you must do the Kosmic Exercises. Space Dimensional Traveler catches a beam of light back to Universe 1 Dimension 4, changes into

Gravity and returns in three light seconds. He marches with the natives, climbs the mountains and performs the Kosmic Exercise. This was a welcoming ritual that opened up a perception portal in Dimensions 11 on Marz.

The Kosmic Exercise

To shine and rise over the night skies, we must do the Kosmic exercise. Birds chirping, waves crashing, big bang drums wasn't by an accident nor a surprise, it's the start of the Kosmic exercise. Four marbles collide, infused in time with universal dimensional lines. The universe moves in rotation on cruise star planets and moons are so amazing. The black hole consumes all in its pathway this formation, unleashes its rath til doomsday. Pulling in the bend of spacetime, the gravitational dj spins, infinitely and simultaneously, on the opposite ends. Expansion got the galaxies dancing. Enhancing comets, moons and other planets pulled by a star that's not too far. Movement rhythm music not human jamming asteroid slamming collision noise fill the black voids with wisdom. Unknown, so we can't describe what lies beyond no vision from our eyes, we must do the Kosmic Exercise!

The Martian wind blows, Mother of All has been entered in code. Mother of All human moon men-hybrids. She was the new mitochondrial marble ball. The first of its kind to fall on the red globe. Her blood will be the royal seed. She breeds with the breeze spreading the first foreign genetics across an alien forest and seas. A new species rises from her womb; the planet Marz is her tomb. The utopia is just a cocoon. As a whispering solar wind blows and holds us all together from within. Space weather on our skin. Mother of all connected all our kin with Martians. Now all earthlings can breathe and believe like Martians. The Kosmic Exercise was just the starting point.

Cosmic stardust is in our hearts. Blood flows like oceans in the dark. Earth flesh to Marz breath. Living with invisible beings, unseen, connecting our strings. She became the Mother of all alien links. Her offspring was earthling space king to moon man, then martian. Perfect genetic ancestry pure chemistry That strain of the DNA chain is too strong to kink. DNA spliced all in between. No gimmicks, all physics and development, no limits. A strain of elements muscles on the skeleton with soul intelligence. Entwined vines in the shape of the double helix. Mother of All biological digits. Her chromosome imprints created visions that can be seen from a distance, her thoughts can be heard in different dimensions, when she speaks her children listen.

"Believe and you will fly in your dreams, visiting unknown, unexplainable Martian physics. New perception, new wisdom. A lesson not guessing our freedom was taken, not given! The sheep are happy living with the chickens," Mother of All said.

She quickly downloaded the code for this information, genetically, and started her own civilization. Space race evolution with the Martian enemy!

Universe 4 / Dimension 10

"Alien Abduction"

Back on Earth, Kozmic Stardust had a fight with time on the inside. It landed him in solitary. He wrote a letter to his friend on the opposite end.

Dear Gravity: Take me to a faraway place voyage through space to an orbit that's more than safe. I'm tired of living in this world today. Let's go beyond just timing. Time is spiraling. I feel like a prisoner on Alcatraz island. Trapped in this fortress. As soon as I get some sunlight, I'm going to absorb it. Heavenly escape with energy into orbit. Traveling dimensionally, I have to go before I forfeit. Pick me up like a forklift. I'm breaking out of this fortress. Meet you on the Exo planet. I'm scrambling! This is it. If you read this, that only means I split. I went along with this script. I'm on the Exo. We have to let go of no standards. No questions, no answers. I'm breaking out before they put me on death row and take me out. I will leave my body, then re-enter while it's in the coroner's van. I need you to go along with this plan. See you on the other side, man. Kozmic Stardust your write hand writing blog man. You See what I did write there? Right?

The plan soon went accordingly. Overdose of something up his nose, he hung a rope, even left a suicide note. The Medical Examiner got blinded by smoke coming from the road. Smoke bombs obstructed his sight as he tried to make a right. Kozmic Stardust gave his body life. In the back of the medical van at the light. Wham bam slam crash! It all happens so fast. Gravity pulls up in a flash. Twice the set up was nice. They escaped from the hands of the land. Off the two flew in Gravity's S-P-A-C-E-S-H-I-P. It was a hybrid matrix.

Gravity said, "Die or take it."

Kozmic stripped naked. Changed his gear and cut his beard. Disguise was weird. Two guys who survive cruising the stars and spheres. Gravity hit a pothole.

Kozmic said, "Not those black hole portals."

The tire popped. They got out to look and began changing the flat. The sky went black. It was an alien attack. The creatures grabbed them with lights from a space plane, their bodies went limp and their souls aboard a space train. Abducted by Dream Car. It was time to see the stars. Kozmic Stardust particles became a living art show.

Dream Car said, "From your mind you will be free. Listen to the soul of your inner galaxy. Uncontrollable thoughts telling you this is me. I'm Dream Car, you must trust this. You have been alien abducted."

Kozmic Stardust says, "I was poked with needles. Left naked in the fetal. Floating in the sky inside an unidentified flying object. Flying alive with the stars and comets I don't know how but now, I remember I was told that I was a member of the Interstellar Dimensional Railroad. Almost a free soul to roam Da Kozmoz. Kozmic Stardust combust, astral projection unknown."

Dream Car said, "After your lessons you can go home mentally and physically. You will be released to your throne spiritually."

His brain wave capacity increased and he had the idea to control his own soul.

"Close your eyes and become your natural being, not human unseen. A piece of time no one can find but you is your mind. Join us roaming globes cruising, spinning, moving, winning. We've been woken up since the beginning, never snoozing," voices from other Interstellar Dimensional Railroads passengers echoed.

Universe 5 / Dimension 9

"The Cold Worlds"

Dropped off on the eldest planet, visiting hybrid android humans first. Then drop below the coldest degrees in the universe. Beautiful frozen worlds are still slowly spinning as frigid winds kill. An arctic life species can start life beneath frozen seas of once liquid steel. Immune to the elements, the oldest settlement still developing like ancient elephants remember this. It's an inhospitable, unfriendly, unwelcoming cold world that gives out the chills.

Dream Car said, "It's a war going on outside. Cherish your life. It's negative one-hundred & forty-six degrees Fahrenheit. Da Kozmoz Publishing, the coldest Ice Storm known. Even when it's froze it doesn't stop. Imagine how cold an ancient parent star glows on top. It's so cold it's hot. It doesn't rot. It's hot and froze. The coldest poem on the globe is what I wrote from my cold world called home. This is the cold shoulder. Still digging for treasure in frozen boulders."

Space Dimensional Traveler buried treasure in his past life off the cliff too heavy to measure width and height, filling books with premium content without the pipe-line. He write-rhymes premium at the right-time. The flow of the snow gave a lifeline! Freezing them cold, holding on to frozen bones leaving gems froze.

Kozmic Stardust is on the block colder than a kelvin. No icepick, just a shovel digging the hustle. It's very much a struggle. Under the trouble of horror trapped in a bubble. Unknown evolution is the revolution of this new mind in design computing. A world floating through a cold tunnel. Both Space Dimensional Traveler and Kozmic Stardust arrive by pure mistake. Frozen in time, they plan their escape. The ice storm trapped both of them in a cube. They floated on a glacier that barely moved.

Space Dimensional Traveler quickly visits another dimension from his last dream. In which he manifested everything he ever needed. It was all there, it appeared to appear, all frozen in ice with him as he reappeared. He realized he couldn't go anywhere. Space Dimensional Traveler then activates natural melanin from within. Kozmic Stardust and Space Dimensional Traveler lie in the ice absorbing, hydrogen and helium. This created a process similar to photosynthesis in himself. Producing a biological change for all the frozen witnesses. Energy transferring the heat to the ice. The Sun goddess siblings shine even brighter than light. They dance in a Kosmic Exercise for life.

Space Dimensional Traveler rises and says, "I felt my skin melt. Flying through the Astro Belt last night. We are burnt ice and our glaciers are on fire. Help!"

Everything and everybody that got trapped in the inhospitable worlds melted. A portal to an additional dimension created from the water production showed itself. Everyone felt it. The gateway to the floods opened up. The ice swung like a drawbridge and a castle raised up behind a moat filled with black holes of danger. No more floating on some ocean with strangers.

Space Dimensional Traveler and Kozmic Stardust entered the makeshift palace; it was an exquisite place.

They fell down below the ocean floor onto the interstellar intrastate.

"Interstellar Interstate 666"

Kozmic Stardust leads the way flying on the highway to hell. Speed limits are gimmicks, no exits just distance. Kosmic Stardust and Space Dimensional Traveler are on the interstellar highway begging for forgiveness.

Kozmic Stardust escapes death and jail cells. You can't tell because he's been sleeping for weeks roaming the streets and galaxies. Unfortunately, Framed for an ice pick killing robbery.

Now he is speeding away from the pain. Flying far in the stars, paying tolls with his soul. Trying to stay out of the flames, he's at the end of his road.

Dream Car said, "Who's not to blame? Racism is embedded in the DNA. Face it, five hundred years of stripping blacks naked, and taking everything, destroying our ancient language. Ain't this some bull? We were the bull with feet and hands that could stand. How can we worship the same god? What are the odds? He would save us?"

Space Dimensional Traveler says, "On Sunday to the Sun Goddess I pray. Each universe is stuck on this one-way, rotational phase, not the calendar or zodiacs that are man made. Forget days, nights, years & decades."

As his third eye mind shines bright as headlights. Kozmic Stardust says, "I'm tired of trying to get my head right. Looking in my rearview, I get a clear view of my entire life. Satan waiting in stripes. It's a demon cartel. Something is burning, no more new car smell. We are at the pitchfork in the road; which way should we go on the highway to hell? It's moving so fast you can't tell. The new world is under that spell. Let's spell s-p-e-l-l."

The highway to hell led them straight to the scorching lava overflow. A massive river of fire contained by flood flames of ice rain. Floods of fake news on the tube are flooding brains. On the highway to hell, stuck in the same lane. Now that's just insane cruising through flames. Nothing to lose if everything is already taken. If you can sleep all day, why wake up? Alarm clock stuck on snooze. I thought I woke up and made a change but got drenched in a wildfire hurricane. Boiling lava flooded this page. Time came to travel on a spacecraft raft and float away on a strange wave.

"The 6th Tunnel Down Below"

What goes up must come down below. Flying higher than Hercules Corona, the massive supernatural galactic superstructure. They both ended up hotter than death valley California. Dried up skull and bones. Up, down and around the Boomerang Nebula is an excellent adventure. Hold on tight. Alien in sight. Submarines can fly from down below. The Interstellar Dimensional Railroad has been identified in flight.

Dream Car says, "They pull you up just enough to drag you back down below."

Kozmic Stardust gets spotted by the police.

"Uh oh Roller coaster. I was abducted by aliens that's not me on that poster," Kozmic said.

Space says, "Aww shucks kid, but I told ya. We were being followed round and round by another Sun high above the clouds. Then back down below the ground. The jail cell, you go. Below hell pass zero. Froze in time one kelvin negative. Two-hundred & seventy-two degrees celsius. They will never let us live or tell us about it."

Cops locked him up and threw away the key that's devilish!

"I surrender; it's like being born blind with owl eyes and deaf with elephant ears. I'm innocent. I escaped to prove my innocence. Sounds weird. Yeah, that's the evidence planted. I can take you back to the selection. But that's irrelevant if I'm telling you. I learned to travel back in time. My dreams become naturally fermented wine as I gradually bend with time. Close your eyes and catch my ride," Kozmic said.

"I've arrived from the hive to pollinate the sector. Alien gorilla bumble bee. Tiny flying ape with bee powers on a flower. In a jungle on a tree. Above a sea of nectar. My honeycomb queen bee I respect her. An army of knitting ants made me a cotton sweater. Boots are all natural leather, no polyester. I'm caged again, but I'm already free. No interruptions except weather. An object in movement moves forever. My mind is balance centered. Blackhole placenta. I can't remember when I passed out and naturally surrendered," Kozmic said.

Everything is something. It's all connected to one thing and that is nothing, but it's something. Disconnected to another dimension, no surprise my exploding stretching is counterclockwise against time. No extension, nothing to hide, but it's an entire dimension hiding inside.

Something is inside something that is alive, a spider with the body of a boa constrictor flies by. A colossal crash guided the big bang in a tiny room full of alien eyes. Tons of dimensions came out of disguise. Kozmic Stardust is just trailing the skies.

Magically, the higher cosmic brain power, solar stardust rain shower space, is a place, but Da Kozmoz is ours. From star to star planets like Marz and Venus. Scenic you can't just dream it, you have to believe it. Unless you believe it. It all starts from a bright room in a fishbowl under a microscope. Stars start to appear in the gloom with a flash of hope.

Kozmic Stardust can't be consumed; he just creates a black hole to escape and moves! Traveling to escape today's pain. Another way to deal with mental and physical pain. To relieve pain first, you must go through pain. You have to truly know what pain is to fully heal.

UNIVERSE 6 / DIMENSION 00

"Koloso Krash"

They go their separate ways lost in a galactic maze. Space Dimensional Traveler visits an old friend. He speeds up back in Time through a supernova explosion in reverse. Traveling back in time as he moves forward in space to meet her Exoplanet planet first. Her soul needs to leave before her planet explodes or is sucked into a black hole. The quest became saving Tess.

Bigger than your imagination. The Milky Way crashed. Andromeda Galaxy smashed. Energetic wavelengths collapsed. The continuum stretches. Expansion again and again. Infinite humongous, infamous fungus simulated in the petri dish above us.

We are descendants of a never ending alien development. Animal cells are telling it. Anything that bang had to start with a crash. A movement just doesn't blast. Extra small to an enormous size. Darkness to life, Kaloso Krash started its own tune, creating Milky Andromeda Boom!

Cosmic fumes ignite an additional dimension. Sparks in another dark room. Deep in dark space, Space Dimensional Traveler enters a brand new galaxy's womb. He made it through the collision gathering hidden wisdom from the alien tomb.

Universe 7 Dimension 4

"Space-Time Continuum"

Time continues on for the Green Goddess. A beautiful young soul lies in bed. Living in her golden years at the age of seventy-seven. A shooting star glides past her window and she makes a wish to the heavens. A strange gravitational pull accompanied by an unknown voice enters. Unknown to the unknown black void. The two then collide, but no noise. At that very moment she dreams of traveling to Da Kozmoz. She then receives the frequencies to leave spiritually. Mother Earth became a pit stop, to the moon, a quick stop off to Marz and back to her room.

Space yells, "Stop! First you must meet the other side of me, Gravity!"

Tess said, "I'm a Hawaiian gypsy, a space traveler since the sixties. What is it you want with me?"

Space shouts, "Come with me!"

He disappears. Gravity appeared out of nowhere. He made nothing into something. Poems into flows.

He said, "I'm Gravity the Space Dimensional Traveler from Da Kozmoz. All this I wrote is raw, untouched hope, pure uncracked yolks, home schooled notes. The galaxy is under construction. Follow me as I combust with the wind. Travel the rush of the galaxy as it spins. From the edge of my skin I dig deep. All this while I daydream or sleep within. I begin yet never end."

No obstructions stood in their way. Off they flew to see the universe in a new way. Visions so clear you can see it from everywhere; uncharted galaxies reappear as others disappear. Unknown so they can't go there for another quintillion light years.

"Oh yeah oh yeah oh yeah! No fear, no fear, no fear," Tess said.

"Escape in your dreams, I truly believe you and I will see! I swear I swear I swear," Space Dimensional Traveler said.

Tess replied, "Wow this is nice. It may extend my life."

"I have traveled to the same dimensions when I sleep. A few hours could literally last for weeks. These dimensions are on a different time scale. Here comes the solar winds, let's sail," Tess said.

Off to the floating continent larger than all the land on earth combined. Surrounded by a sea of molten gold and silver. The creatures with human features kinda look familiar.

Space Dimensional Traveler said, "Who could say no to a new companion? Time is stretching and expanding. Time and travel is mind travel. Your choice of vehicle. Very few have this gift, a shift, a wave of energy between places exchanging movement arrangements. You're very friendly."

Tess said, "The shift began for me while living in Hawaii for many years. I moved home to NE. It was time to disappear. I've traveled the world hoping it wouldn't end. Then I came across a new friend. Everything became more revealing and I became more focused and my mind opened. I have been flying in the dark for so long. Going along with the experience of living two lives, one on earth, the other in the sky. It's been 60 years. I am wise. So much wisdom to share but no one seems to care. I'm glad you are here."

After a quintillion light years they enter a new world in an extra dimension. The cove smelled of moon flowers. They rose over a steep hill. The grassy trail became a brick road. The two flew above flying high like a car off a cliff. They saw bloody red city streets. Strange dark red concrete, a red rose, a rose diamond, a heart shaped stone. This place was weird, it sure wasn't home.

Space realized clouds rolled into perpetual grayness. Spirals of expression are ancient lessons. All Built upon each other in fright. The exit was in sight. They raced in the sky above the dark caves without light.

Tess said, "Now you must meet my other side." She disappears in the sky.

All of a sudden, everything that wasn't, became something. Beautiful clothes, royal robes, golden thrones. A hidden castle, a secret home of the Green Goddess, her royal highness. She showed Space the way to universal balance. Both flew back in time to 12/ 12/ 1212 12:12 am and stayed till 12:12pm. Only to realize Time doesn't exist, it's simply the distance traveled from point to point.

The Green Goddess said, "I'm Tess on the opposite end, just like Gravity is your parallel twin. I must return to my quest. Nice to meet you, Space Dimensional Traveler. Take care of Tess." She disappears as Tess reappears.

It was time for Tess to get back to the bottom of the food chain. A retired elder. Just arrived from Hawaii, she took a doze off and woke up froze to a bench in a storm of hail balls. She had nothing but basic bare necessities. Trying to rest at ease. Traveling abroad overseas harmed her knees. This was her last journey, but when she sleeps, her dreams become the easiest way to be free. Free from years of belly dancing. Free from rocking hard. Free from rebellion, a rebel Hawaiian rocking hippie, traveling gypsy. Free from limits. She learned that life has infinite possibilities and wisdom with high capacity capabilities. She sighs and goes back to the current time.

Tess cries and says, "Hopefully I see you on the other side."

She lives in North Eastern America. Surrounded by farmers and mosquitoes with malaria. Neighbors arm themselves for the coming war. A world war on the American shore.

"My sister walked away from this life. How could she leave me colder than ice? My service dog passed before I left Hawaii. My life has been full of loss and anxiety. Full of pain and grief. It has taken a toll on my spirit and me. I have to say goodbye again to my late loved family and friends one last time. As we travel forward back in time I will see them once more on the timeline. Again, I hope to see you on the other side, my friends."

Universe 8 Dimension 3

"The Greatest Invention Ever"

Kozmic Stardust approaches the bench as he represents himself in court. His life hangs in the balance on the fence, everything went silent. Homegrown defense.

"Your Honor, Time cries with sorrow because it knows of no hope tomorrow. Life is full of time borrowed. Madness is packaged in. The devil is trying to put a date on my fate because of his racist hate. Let's make Universe 8 great. I became the target like a new world slave sent away to an early grave. I saw a tear drop go down the clock and time cries, but it never dies or stops. The fourth dimension is weeping morning, noon and evening. What are the three reasons? What do you believe in? What's your sequence? Are you a demon? Why are you leaving? Time is screaming revealing true secrets. It only hides in between lengths. Face it, Don't waste it. Your time is fading and erasing. Earth is a sacred spaceship, don't get trapped in the…… What I'm saying is, I'm innocent listen to this. If I was the killer with the ice pick, how could I feed my wife and kids? My only connection to the crime scene is the officer that pulled behind me. If the killer struck six miles down a froze road, how could I have traveled on all that snow. I'm not that type of guy I was snowed in with my family. That's my alibi. With an entire state of emergency, the only vehicles traveling urgently are the authorities, otherwise I would be seen. All the evidence collected was in a duffle bag. Double wrapped I guarantee my fingerprints don't match. But may I suggest you check the camera on his dash? He waited a mile and half back. After he shoveled a path to the underpass. I noticed the tall grass was unbothered from the snow, as I pulled over to the dry shoulder. Guess where I was at? When the officer showed his badge, he was carrying a duffel bag that he grabbed from the tall grass. It must have been previously stashed. As he asked for a license registration insurance check the procurance. I noticed it traveling back through time, returning from my past. Officer already had the bag. All he needed was a man that was black," Kozmic said.

The jury finds the officer guilty with no doubt. The lead juror sings, "Crime time! You can make time, you can take time, you can face-time but you can't fake it this time, your time dies."

The honorable judge of Universal law speaks, "Your life is priceless fibers and threads, spiders and legs. They act like I'm trying to squeeze diamonds out of a rising climate. Time waits for no one, you're born then dead. You can kill time, you can waste time, you can spend time but you can't save time, unless you're blessed to fly right beside time. Time flies. Poker is bluff time, fourth quarter crunch time. Hungry? Well wait for lunchtime. Work shouldn't be a fun time. Arrest that officer, he must pay with his time. I saw enough hate crimes."

Kozmic speaks outside at a podium when he leaves the courthouse, "Time flies, when you are having fun, it's the illusion in the sky, not the sunrise. Time is money. We are forever in debt to political influence until death. It was designed, to supervise, our lives, hypnotize,& divide, a substance, of nothing, to keep us blind. Demons and reptiles are just a minuscule piece of the alien government. Time is a memorable distance, let's take advantage of this!"

UNIVERSE 9 DIMENSION 2

"Traveling Teamwork makes the Dreamwork"

Faster than a hypersonic Intercontinental ballistic nuclear mixture compressed in a missile of fission and fusion, this world becomes a mirror reflection of itself rather than an illusion.

It seems Space Dimensional Traveler, Kozmic Stardust and the Green Goddess joined together in their dreams. They visit the Space Race. Kosmic needed to see the Mother of All's face. A glimpse of the future human race. Is what he needs to witness, then he can wake up and accept his country's forgiveness. Space and the Green

Goddess just wanted life to call it living. Flying high in the distance, all the travelers are winning.

Tunneling through Da Kozmoz, they go faster than a speeding missile. Mental powers appearing physical. Energetic electronic pulses from each traveler's brainpower provide atmospheric creations. Hidden visuals begin to appear. A mix of analogue and digital equations began to form, near. All this is taking place and no one is here. They're already halfway to Marz without a care.

Back on Mother Earth; Tess is fast asleep after an intense internet search. She rested deeply. Up all night she kept getting sleepy. Kozmic Stardust proved his innocence and gained his freedom. No more chains, no more pain but nothing will ever be the same. Who's 2 Blame? We don't need them. Gravity daydreams of something he reads Sol on Marz his second release on the streets. He knew Space Dimensional Traveler was who set him free.

Universe 2 Dimension 1

"Mothership"

Gravity returned to Mothership. Her hair grew leaves. She loved to hug the trees. Her feet grew roots entangled in her every step. Her eyes are bright enough to light up the sky. When she blinks, the sky gets dark. She breathes life into every breath. She speaks from the heart. She Grabbed his hand. The dolphins swam, carrying twins on their heads, one on each side of her breast as they rest.

Mothership says, "Pick one and restart again. Join your friends. You are most faithful just as your father once was before he reached the point of no return. Now go learn a new way to earn another life turn."

Gravity remained in the same clothes.

Mothership shouted, "No, that's the same road your father chose!"

Gravity chose both twins, hoping his plan would balance out in the end. Gravity has a different approach. In his dreams he clones his soul. Space Dimensional Travelers and he were one of their own. A separate identity, two new entities. The two could actually breathe and walk the same street. No more entanglement on the opposite end of the universe and one on Earth. Both could stand side by side. Gravity's choice to divide was the first. Now it's two back on Mother Earth and two entangled somewhere in some far universe. Two new characters we have yet to see.

"Space Dimensional Traveler be careful the next time you sleep it's guaranteed you'll meet your new friend to be. He could be your enemy," Mothership said.

Before Mothership winked her eyes and tossed the two guys in the sky, she had a surprise.

She Shouted, "Gravity you chose wisely! There is a key in your future. It opens the true surprise. Glad I didn't lose you. Be careful when you fly close to this new guy or you won't be the only traveler who can play both sides!"

Off they went, Mothership wisdom and gifts are beyond heaven sent.

Space Dimensional Traveler speaks to Gravity for the first time on the same timeline.

He said, "Thanks for releasing me to be here. Finally, close and near. When I was your inner traveler, we did it all. Now you've brought me to your world, let's have a ball."

Gravity replies, "Don't forget we multiplied. There are two others now on the other side. Wow, it's really a surprise. I wonder who these guys are and how far away their stars are."

"I miss my home already. The Jungle Star System," Space Dimensional Traveler said.

" Are you ready? Alright grab my hand and hold steady," Gravity said.

Universe 10 Dimension 2

"Celestial Celestine"

On Mother Earth Tess shares her wisdom with her only family member left alive she found by luck online. A soul in disguise a different race, same bloodline.

Returning from her last trip, Tess updates her status and location. [I'm not sure if this world can handle me. I'm lost in my mind, racing through either time or insanity!] She posted this all across her social media quick. Tess searched for more friends and family. After requesting a few locals, she received universal amnesty in an inbox from a picture-less profile. Can it be? The message read: Don't poison your mind with the booklet. It's not candy. That's how the monsters get inside. Even the blind can see the bull under the bed. It's trying to hide in our heads. Look up in the sky, it's a bird, it's a plane. It's a demon feeding your brain a full list of games. Fear keeps you near and never aware of what's really there. It never was fair, but who really cares? It's all fallacies! Why watch what you eat and count calories? Most food comes from sour seeds that were modified genetically. Divided states of monsters and demons that keep effective control with pills & synthetic trees. Meaning the naïve becomes the next breed of beast that feeds on the weak in the streets, every day of the week. I'm your great niece. I'm the one who woke you up on the beach, when you almost froze in your sleep. I smacked you with a cold breeze. I'll see you in a week. So stay out of the nervous system. It's run like a circus to keep the workers working for no purpose. You can win, let's go cosmic surfing! No catfish please, I sure hope you're the right person.

Tess replies with her address and location. A week later, she receives a knock on the door. The stars were in rotation for sure. It was her German relative Celestial Celestine and her German shepherd Neptune on the scene. They instantly hugged and began talking under the moon sharing dreams. After the meal, the two made a deal. Tess was ready to travel some more. Then it was revealed they met on the other side before.

Déjà vu! They had been here before the two knew what to do. They held hands while sleeping, floating above the waterbed. Fingers interlocked, hair hanging in the air. Cosmic energy ex spelled out everywhere.

The trip began when Celestial Celestine waved energy throughout Da Kozmoz. The energetic radiant angel moved the planets as if they needed a checkup for a runny nose. She tilted them. Spun some faster. Slowed others down with her laughter. She removed objects before impact. Clogging black holes with celestite to keep them intact. She enjoyed healing entire universes. Tess did not know her abilities until she witnessed Celestial Celestine at work, checking universes health. Tess and Neptune began checking planets for proper rotation and giving out moons. Reusing objects saved before collision. Neptune runs on rings chasing his own tail around frozen worlds. Life starts to sprout all throughout universe after universe with wisdom. Celestial Celestine healings worked. They both woke up back on Earth.

Celestine says, "I know Pyrite isn't fools gold. The chase for gold takes control of the soul. If you chase the carrot, you get dragged into the rabbit hole."

Off to dream off to sleep off to the stars above the street. In a world beyond your reach Tess & Celeste flew to the edge of the universe to relax on the cosmic beach. Tess & Celestine daydreamed of; **The Ship and Silver Seas:**

(Journal entry 28,123)

We dreamt of standing on the bow of a ship. It was icy cold. The furs We had on were comforting against the cut of the wind. But the sight of the water was spellbinding. It was silver, shiny and moved in undulations like mercury. The sky was icy blue. We passed small islands and pieces of land jutting out into the water. No cities but other smaller boats traveling the other way. Then we heard small sounds, like fairy bells tinkling. In the water, there were small crystal icebergs. Made of silver water, they reflected like rainbows and made sounds when brushing against the ship. We were on the ship for many days, flowing through the musical waters. The air became warmer as we traveled along an Archipelago. No signs of people or small coastal towns. The water was changing to a golden hue as it became warmer. We docked at a small port. The tropical perfume surrounding me welcomed me in. I felt embraced by this island. We woke up yearning to return. That day I walked up the valley into the deep forest. A forbidden path, known to local people only. Seeking sanctuary. I bathed in the queen's pools, seeking comfort and cleansing. I Gathered mangos and macadamia nuts from the sacred trees. I was still wondering about my dreams. What they were I did not know. What we knew was that we were ancient Alien Indigo.

Tess wrote in her notes the second she woke.

Universe -2 Dimension -99

"Nightmare Car"

"I never thought I would create my symphony. My DNA, my history, the past, toward fast forward forever now til infinity passing down my traits and chemical alien energy. Remember me in your fondest memory," Anti-Gravity said.

Diablo aliens sailing in from the depths of hell. With scrolls printed on gold to spread disease across all globes, stories were neither read nor told. Not an oracle, not a divine Diablo alien in the sky. An unidentified flying train. Alien creatures with red skin but human features. That wasn't from here.

Anti-Gravity said, "Take me to your leader and come here."

He used his fingers in the air. Started drawing pictures like an artist. Sent to target all evil ways to use technology. To be the smartest in the galaxy.

(Pointing to the Jungle Star System.)

Anti-Gravity said, "Pay attention, follow me. I'm a Space Dimensional Traveler's worst enemy. Take me there at once or pay with your fronts!"

The Interstellar Dimensional Railroad space train car said, "That's not how it works on this ride. You will earn your time, but first you must perform everlasting duties to even reach the other side."

"You may be smart but you're trapped in this space train car until you're released back to your physical body. I'm your new consciousness, your leader, your chief, your daddy and mommy. I will telepathically inform you of what is needed of you. Copy? Your intelligence will only make things harder for yourself. I'm your new belief. Now allow me to introduce myself. I'm the Nightmare

Car, the last car to balance all the other positive cars before me. I'm the one and only negative charge. I'm strong enough to wipe out an entire star system from very far," Nightmare car said.

"Allow me to speak, I'm Anti-Gravity. A dangerous connection to the end of the multiverse, the last frontier, the edge of Da lab," Anti-Gravity said.

Another voice spoke calmly. It wasn't a zombie.

"I'm Unidimensional Ground. I don't belong here. Me and my inner self got mixed up. He belongs inside but instead he's in total control of my physical body. All I can do is communicate to him in these nightmares he has. I wonder if you guys can help me find him on the other side, he goes by the name of Kozmic Stardust. He stole my soul from Mothership a billion years ago," Unidimensional Ground said.

"Adding to your pain Let's start your first day off on Planet Rock. Before Invisible Energy silently nudges it into universal black hole tombs for punishment. So you can feel destruction running through your new cosmic veins. You guys will have to save the robotic cows from the solar tycoon before he makes them surrender during their last jump over the moon," Nightmare Car said.

Anti-Gravity said, "Wow this is insane, Invisible Energy is my twin's son! This is not a game!"

UNIVERSE 12 DIMENSION 328

"Jungle Star System"

A wonderful young Tri-star system that supports massive Goldilocks zones. It had worlds drenched with aquatic life. Several planets hid in the brightness in between and behind the growing stars. These three stars chase each other in a cosmic dance spectacle. Wolf, Sheep and Dog shine so bright the nearby planets never see night. From Mother Earth they shine as one the three sisters to the Sun.

Gravity and Space Dimensional Traveler arrive on planet five and the Space Dimensional Traveler realizes this isn't the place he saw when he was just a thought in Gravity's mind. It was even better from his own thoughtful design. He was better than home. Space Dimensional Traveler was free to roam and be his own.

Gravity spotted a forest full of speakers and microphones. World five was just outside the daylight line. one of the few visible from afar. Just under five light years to reach Marz. "Now that I know how to get home, let's go check on the evolution of the space race," Space Dimensional Traveler said.

Gravity said "We can't go yet haven't you noticed the sheep star is trapped in between wolf and dog stars. It is constantly pulsating dark energy fighting for a new orbital position. That's the last electromagnetic wave we need to research for our connection to the Lost Galaxy of the Pulsar Star."

Space Dimensional Traveler says, "Wait this is it, the galaxy we seek is Invisible Energy being pushed by Dark Energy. They are your son's and that's moving you Gravity.

"I told them not to play too close to the Pulsar Star! It's the invisible source to it all," Gravity said.

Space Dimensional Traveler asked, "How are they still moving you?"

"You've only seen what they can do in this dimension," Gravity laughed out loud.

A quick drift from the solar wind bouncing off of planet six. Gravity rode the dip and took a trip to Dimension 11 real quick.

Universe 3 Dimension 11

"Space Race Developed"

As Space & Grav entered the Martian atmosphere, the Indigenous were performing a spring rain dance. This was their chance.

May the stars carry your sadness away from night till day let us pray. Spiral galaxy days is the first stance to complete the solar rain dance. Hope it's healing and the Sun Goddess is revealing, concealing the pain away from the acid rain stains. Space Dimensional Traveler describes Mother of All on the mainframe. Teaching arriving Earthlings what they need to remain the same. Maintaining the brain is the head of the chain!

She says, "The clouds drift away. The thunder rumbles are the forecast prediction of what's coming in. Strikes of lightning from a distance. The wolf howling is forgiveness. All natural nothing comes within. The sky goes into universal darkness and the space race family wins. The planet spins from start to end. Solar stance begins a dance for the plants. The drought and the dry lands. East to West, Indigenous Martians Move the route in all directions, North to South. Invisible Energy flows through like a river of chemistry. From left to right reflections, the majestic mountains erect stars and trees. No need to intervene on a level unseen. A cool rain and a breeze."

Time has never disturbed Indigenous culture, hidden compounds unaltered blurred words. They never thought they would have found an ancient Martian burial ground, still in its Aboriginal condition with no living witness around.

Mother of All sets up her newfound campground outside a tomb without a sound. Now or the past, life goes up and down. Moving to the sound of cosmic hearts. Ignited by lightning, a spark opened up the tomb. An identified reddish copper brown alien-like man rose from the quicksand. They stopped the solar dance, when Ancient Martian spiritual leaders entered the cosmic room. They Spoke in volumes of a trillion speakers. Providing knowledge of a million leaders, tranquility, no interference, pure ability with ancient rain dance capabilities. Loud thunder strikes of electricity and acid rain flood the valley as the pristine clean alien beings begin to sing. (hmmmmmm hmmmmmm)

"Thoughts are worth more than words. Keep selling your dreams, somebody has to believe. Time to learn telepathy! First, my ancestors were over there on the blue globe, but we finally made it back home. I'm here disappearing and reappearing from the rear. Crystal clear Invisible Energy gives telepathy. His story was never fair, a great friend to me. The humans really started as martians right there. Knowledge of self is returned. Common sense isn't quite clear. That's quite weird. The original woman has returned! Allow me to share! I heard sound waves moving faster than a light year in my right ear. Cruising after time despite fear. Leave all your bad times behind. Close your eyes. Become what's inside. Feel your destiny information about the star design density. Close your eyes and find your destiny," Mother of All said.

They find themselves in Universe 1 Dimension 3.

Universe 1 Dimension 3.

Science is M-I-N-D. Mind is chemistry. Imagination is a gift endlessly. The travelers are in high gear quite far yet quite near. Energy passed invisibly, yet physically can be you and me. They escaped this dangerous trap. Experi-M-E-N-T-A-L-Y. In Universe 1 Dimensions 1-4. More thoughts left the temple. Now that they're free from internal prison, They can really get some space, but wait! Experiment M-I-N-D is space & space is M-I-N-E.

Mother of All says, "Class come back to meditate. Don't waste your time. Now entangle your dreams from both sides to escape time which has never existed. Your mind holds the vision. Let's take a visit. I promise we won't go far. It's time for Da Kozmoz team to travel beyond Marz."

Gravity joins them before they leave. The elders all point to him to begin the travel story. He points to the hidden Pulsar star, the hidden heart. The fire blew out and his story was told in the dark. The wolves howl, the wind churns; they all gather hands in a circle sitting around a flame-less pit yet it still burns. Gravity makes a wish and the fire is lit. Now everyone loosens their grip and takes the trip, as the elder Martians play the drums.

"As long as life revolves around the sun. The knife can be solved with the gun. We shall develop with the sound of the drum, bum, bum, bum.

"It's a bit unorthodox on that third rock. They need an alien psychologist and a robotic biologist," a young Martian said.

Bum, bum, bum goes the drum, drum, drum. The circle of souls rises above their bodies; they blast off like a spaceship.

"Why search outer space when my soul is outer space? A solar gas spaceship right in our faces. Time has been riding the orbit line since the beginning of time," Gravity said.

"The second we used our brains and wrote on the walls of caves the second dimension came. Earth is the first world, the third is the globe. Our inner souls are the second connection to Da Kozmoz. Passing stars far beyond ours spin the bottle in a death spin copy paste print thoughts as a weapon the universe marbles forever stretching," said a Martian.

Bum, bum, bum a Martian beat the drum, drum, drum.

Universe 2 Dimension Unknown

"The Lost Galaxy of the Pulsar Star"

Gravity and Space Dimensional Traveler completed the mission. They found the pulse of the multiverse and connected human birth to the lost galaxy subconsciously throughout each universe and dimension they traveled. Kozmic Stardust is connected. Invisible Energy is much respected. That was the end of the battle. Little did they know it was one universe & one dimension they missed. Universe 11 Dimension 99 was next on their list. Deep beneath the microwave background a new story embedded itself without a sound.

Outroduction

Once upon a time in a universe far away a keyboard had a best friend, a mouse. A push and a click over and over again. A lyrical design, a miracle hidden in disguise inside ancient Martian alien minds. The demons from the darkside have misaligned old information into unknown names. The Great Sleeping Pill, all the planets scrambled in the skies and jumped out of line.......

Mothership said, "Look Gravity you're not done, writing till you write a book son. Chop and boil and mix medication with food dude. Bring it to a boil and keep it bubbling at 312 degrees, drain and cover with foil. Then serve breakfast."

Nightmare Car said, "Park up on the avenue to spark a fuse. Don't do what you need to do. Money is the root to all evil. Don't stand like a man, your plan is see through. You are so tragic that you belong with maggots. Stop writing, nobody is liking or likes this. Keep it top secret, stop reaching. No more conspiracy theories, you've reached the demons now the surviving angels are screaming."

Gravity & Space simultaneously replied, "It already happened! We lived to witness the final chapter. This isn't written; it's happening in the opposite fashion, a parallel universe mashup. Now it's two Gravitational Pull Masters!"

"Time is the distance traveled to a place in space. Most people can't remember how they became a member of something so awake. To live is to exist within orbit. The universe is infinite galaxy marbles clashing against each other absorbing, galactic organs, fantastic & horrible forfeits. Kosmic Stardust flows within we. The Parallel Universe hides in poetry," Da Kozmoz said.

"With Space Dimensional Traveler, Invisible Energy, Dark Energy & Gravity as the Soul specimens of my latest science project. The Parallel Universe is connected to Da Kozmoz's fishbowl. A pure entanglement between

the two can't be denied. It's the Gravitational bloodline!"
Great Grandmother Universe replied.

Cosmic mathematicians travel fast. Performing the task of calculating a hidden signal in a new law of physics. Brainwaves are built from the position of Mother Earth during an interstellar light transmission. Many childbirths received the galaxy's frequencies from the Alien Indigo seed. A new species that leads to connecting and respecting the solar breeze. The Parallel Universe speaks, spins, breathes, it's you, it's me!

"Eyes are windows to the gold. Melanin is the birth of the soul. This is getting old," Da interstellar biologist whispers as she types in a code.

[dakozmoz.com] were the keys she typed in. Life as we know it began. A restart on the same simulation but this time on the opposite end. Just for the sake of the Alien Indigo parallel connection, an awesome lesson and a tremendous task in Da Lab with Great Grandmother Universe's blessing!

To be continued.................

"Da Kozmoz"

Poetic Motion from the Stars

(The End is The Beginning)

Written by **Gravity Gravitational Pull**

Secret hidden ending is the start of a new beginning!!!

Universe11 Dimension 99

(THE END IS THE BEGINNING)

Gravity and Space Dimensional Traveler take a break, fall asleep and wander space.

Anti-Gravity and Undimensional Ground arrive on the lethal Planet Rock as it moves through dimensions of the past. Rock human hybrids tried to live through the blast. Artificial intelligence became trapped in cows jumping over buildings then moons in a flash. No matter what, Planet Rock was consumed into black hole tombs during the crash.

Undimensional Ground, realizes he can go back in time just like they traveled to Dimension 521,801. He decides to use his newfound knowledge of Da Kozmoz and revisits Mothership a billion years ago; at the same time Kozmic Stardust is being transferred into the body that he was truly destined for. At first he can't watch, then he interrupts and takes control of the baby Mothership holds. Kozmic Stardust is then forced into the mind. Unidimensional Ground solved his own problem, really quick from one lesson. He became free to rome Da Kozmoz. Nightmare Car had no choice but to release him from his duties.

They both realize the lesson and appear in a room full of colossal crash fumes. Hollow bags of doom appear in the air. Boom! The two wake up and laugh. Gravity and Space just met their other halves on the other side of the tall grass.

Now Space needs a new form of travel or he can never go back. It was time for the spiritual battle. A miracle or what have you. Gravity knew what he had to do. Meditate to elevate.

Gravity thought out loud, "If I set things straight. put everything on the plate. Never hesitate. Why would I wait? Dream high stakes and live life. No mistake can be made if you breathe, right? It's time to lead beyond the light!"

Sitting Copperskin Indian style. He closed his eyes, became a six year old child and smiled. Dreaming calmly, he witnessed the battle above the clouds interstellar wild.

Young Gravity magically orbits Universe11 Dimension 99 and sees Nightmare car and his other future half; Anti-Gravity, picking up Space Dimensional Travelers' new form of travel. He couldn't wait to see.

Kozmic Stardust appears, which was weird, he was there. He held a key that was given to him by Mothership.

It jumped from his hand and became another kid. His face was dark, stars began to spark, the air became fair. He was shaped like a bear with human hair. Top Knotch galactic gear covered him like a shield of technology.

He said two words, "Follow me."

Nightmare Car takes Anti-Gravity aboard and Young Gravity follows behind. Young Gravity follows behind far enough not to annihilate the entire fishbowl by coming in contact with his future half.

The human alien/space bear headed straight to the Asteroid Belt. The Top Knotch gear seems to have been pre-programmed for a specific planet. Music seems to be playing as he gets closer to Pluto; even more jamming as he approaches Jupiter. He reaches the asteroid belt and orbits a globe known as Judeau Da Planet.

The huge speaker in his Top Knotch gear screams, "Big Proph, Da Reaper home!"

Undimensional Ground got his physical body back. Kozmic Stardust was trapped. Space dimensional Traveler jumped inside the mind of the space/alien bear. The Top Knotch A.I. gear disappeared; it was no longer there.

Stay tuned for more Kosmic Konnections

Coming soon from Da Kozmoz Publishing

Judeau Da Planet

A Soul on Earth Lives Beyond a Sol On Marz

written by

Judeau Da Planet

2022 Da Kozmoz Publishing

.

Invisible Energy

Under the Fishbowl

Written by
Gravity Gravitational Pull

2022 Da Kozmoz Publishing

Transparently Solid

The Unknown Scripture

Written by

Mer Trapo
&
Gravity Gravitational Pull

2022 Da Kozmoz Publishing

www.ingramcontent.com/pod-product-compliance
Lightning Source LLC
Chambersburg PA
CBHW080743250626
47162CB00010B/3008